The Reporter and the Penguin

Steve Martaindale

To Donna
+ Vern

Never stop exploring!

DEDICATION

To the one who encouraged me to work in Antarctica,
who emboldened me to attempt writing my stories, the
goodness in my life, to my Leah.

CONTENTS

ACKNOWLEDGMENTS

It took me longer than many journalists to decide I wanted to write a book. By that time, more than a hundred different people had come and gone as co-workers in several different small newspapers. I had also lived and worked in a number of incredibly different towns and interacted with an unimaginable number of people.

Of immeasurable importance to this story was the opportunity to work as a journalist with the U.S. Antarctic Program, which, I should probably say, neither reviewed nor approved this novel. There, I met the most amazing collection of people possible in one contained environment. All of these elements influence, to varying degrees, the fictitious towns and characters which make up "The Reporter and..." stories.

One thing a reporter learns: "Everyone has a story."

1 AN OPPORTUNITY

Shane Peltzer grumbled while securing his extreme cold weather gear, deliberately ignoring the stares of his co-workers, and headed out into a merciless Antarctic wind ripping unabated across the expansive Ross Ice Shelf.

It wasn't incredibly cold, by local standards, maybe minus 20 degrees Fahrenheit, but the strong winds stung a spot on his face where it found exposed skin.

The blowing snow made it difficult to see the end of the sled they called a living room during the traverse, but once he got there he found the first flag where it should be. Still mumbling about his co-workers, he set out, as he had every evening on this slow trip into the Antarctic interior, walking toward the large workshop sled that carried the equipment for which he was responsible.

He followed the line of flags and eventually realized there were no more, nor was his sled where it should be. More aware of his white-out surroundings, he continued a few more feet ... maybe it was farther; it was hard to tell ... and the conditions continued to deteriorate. He couldn't see the sled now unless he tripped over it.

Disoriented, he tried to retrace his steps but could not tell where he had been. He couldn't see the ground and if he could, his tracks would already be filled in by blowing snow. At this point, he was not sure what direction was camp.

For just a moment, he yelled obscenities toward the other members of the expedition, quite sure they purposely moved or misplaced flags to cause him grief. Someone's going to hear about this, he promised.

As his rage died, he realized he really was lost, forcing him to pause and consider his situation. He couldn't be far from camp. His clothing would provide enough protection from the cold for a good while. He could either try to dig into the snow enough for a little protection from the wind or keep looking for camp. Besides, the others were probably coming after him already if, indeed, it was only a stupid joke. While he did not get along with any of them, they wanted only to embarrass him, not do any harm. Yes, that's true, he assured himself.

He chose to continue moving in widening circles in hopes of stumbling across someone or something. He concentrated on staying the course, continuing in a circle but steadily expanding it.

Suddenly, the snow and ice gave way and he experienced the sheer terror of falling into nothingness, only to pass out when the descent abruptly ended.

When he came to, the only thing he could feel was an intense pressure on his chest, making each breath small and unbelievably difficult. It took a few seconds before he realized he fell into a crevasse – a crack in the ice often obscured by a thin layer of snow.

You hear about such dangers and you learn to watch for them, but that's nearly impossible in whiteout conditions. And, to be honest, he had given in to his anger and ignored safety.

He struggled a bit, to no avail. Each movement made breathing more difficult.

The reality of his situation overwhelmed him. Nobody knew his exact location and he's heard the stories. They do not expect to find your body. Even if they did, extracting it would be next to impossible and prove dangerous to others.

On the good side, he thought with surprising calm, considering the cold and his diminishing oxygen intake ... it won't take long.

SEPTEMBER 14, 7:58 A.M.

JP Weiscarver wiggled as he tried to get comfortable in a folding metal chair in the makeshift newsroom of the Oldport Odds and Ends. He needed to crank out some busy work before hitting the streets for a 9 a.m. interview with a local man commissioned to provide a sculpture for the state capitol.

"It'll be nice to write a story that has nothing to do with Hurricane Clarice," he mumbled.

"What's that, JP?" The question came from Lifestyles editor Pat Baird, who didn't wait for an answer. "You're here early."

"Maybe, but it's definitely late for you, isn't it?"

"Well, since the hurricane kicked us out of our regular digs, getting here early just isn't as much fun. I mean, the circulation crew is even operating out of a different building. I'm ready for us all to get together again."

"I guess that's what I was muttering when you came in," JP said. "I have an interview this morning that has nothing to do with the hurricane and I'm excited about it."

"Good luck with that," interjected city editor Stanley Hopper, who entered the room lugging two laptop computers. "I thought everything was about Hurricane, uh..."

"Clarice," the other two said simultaneously.

"Honestly, Stanley," Pat continued, "this will be the biggest story of your career. The least you can do is remember the name of the storm."

"I do know I got tired of reading in every story this

morning that today marks one month since it hit. Hurricane Clarice, Clarice, Clarice," he repeated en route to the table serving as his desk.

SEPTEMBER 14, 11:33 A.M.

While walking to his pickup after completing the interview, JP saw he had a text message from the cops and courts reporter. The work they did leading up to and following the hurricane had further cemented a strong partnership with Jennifer O'Hanlon. They made a good team and pressed each other to do better reporting.

Jennifer answered her phone on the first ring.

"Mr. Hopper wants to know if you can have your feature story ready to go today. Please say yes or else he'll have me do another hurricane recovery angle."

"Good morning to you, too. Yeah, Cole arrived just before I left and is hanging around to take some photos. I can have the story ready in no time; it's just not what I wanted it to be."

"Do I need to warn Mr. Hopper?"

"No, it's just me. The sculptor, who's apparently lived here in Oldport all his life without anybody knowing about him, will do a piece to be placed on the grounds of the state capitol."

"That sounds good."

"Sure and I'll make a fine story out of it. Between you and me, it kind of bummed me out when he said the statue will be a tribute to the heroes of Hurricane Clarice. I know, I know, I'm overreacting, but if I don't start putting a little distance between me and that hurricane, I might go crazy. Just a second. Hmm, I'm getting a call from the 720 area code. Where's that?"

"Don't know. Later."

"Hello," JP said while sliding into his yellow truck and extracting a pen and notepad.

"JP Weiscarver? This is Sally Hutchens with the U.S.

Antarctic Program. Are you still interested in working in Antarctica?

SEPTEMBER 14, 2:22 P.M.

"Hey, boss, I've got a problem," JP said to his city editor.

"It's kinda late for you to be bailing on the sculptor feature, Weiscarver."

"No, story and photo are ready. The problem is more personal."

"Then the shrink is out."

"Hey, it affects you, too, boss."

"Then I'm all ears, but make it quick."

"We talked about my applying to work a season in Antarctica."

"Yeah, 'cause of a story you did about a college professor who went up there."

"Down there. And I didn't get the job, but they made me first alternate and had me go through all the physical testing and everything. Remember?"

"Don't like where this is going, Weiscarver."

"I got a call this morning. One of the three folks they hired 'freaked out,' according to the boss lady. Now, they want me. But it has to be pretty much immediately. The journalists are scheduled to deploy Sept. 29."

"So, you have a couple of weeks."

"Not really, boss. If I'm going to be gone more than four months, I have arrangements to make, no small amount of shopping and packing to do and I cannot head overseas without going home to visit my folks. Plus, I have to report to Denver for training prior to departure. So, the question is, are you still OK with me taking a leave to do this, like, right away? When we talked about it earlier, we were living a happy coastal life in a town not ravaged by a Category 5 hurricane."

"Son," Stanley said, stopping everything and looking JP

in the face, "there's never a good time for something like this, but I guarantee you an experience of a lifetime. All kidding aside, I would do whatever we have to do to give you this chance."

"Boss, that's touching."

"Don't get used to it. Here's the deal. I already cleared this with Margaret last June, so I'll update her and bring Ed Roberts into the conversation. You will have a job when you get back, but I want one thing from you. Send us a weekly report and maybe a photo. We'll create a standing Sunday feature, 'Oldport's connection to the bottom of the world,' or something like that. Maybe that'll keep all your little old lady fans from hassling me about not seeing your byline all winter. And, by all means, make sure you include penguins. People seem to love 'em."

JP seemed dizzied by the rapid chain of events.

"Weiscarver? You OK?"

"Wow. Looks like I'm going to Antarctica."

SEPTEMBER 14, 5:12 P.M.

Bubba, JP's pet ferret, acted as if he had won a trip to Disney. He scurried around piles of clothes and jumped into and out of boxes, pausing briefly to play with his toy ball or JP's shoe laces.

"Don't go sneaking off with any of my stuff, Bubba. I don't have time to play hide-and-seek. I wonder if you'll miss me while I'm gone."

Busy as the ferret was, he still pumped it up to a new level when the doorbell rang. JP could barely hold him as he answered the door.

"You, you ... I cannot come up with the appropriate label for you right now."

"Jennifer, I'm sorry, but ..."

"You're sorry? For what? For leaving me, for leaving us, to deal with this hurricane recovery without you or for saying nothing about it until you're practically walking out the door?"

JP laughed at that.

"The latter, only," he said. "I'm happy to put hurricane coverage behind me for a while. It'll still be here when I get back. Look, here comes Guy."

"Don't try to change the subject to pizza. Did you order enough for me?"

"Howdy, folks," the pizza delivery guy chimed in as he approached. "Y'all are hitting the pie a little early this evening."

"I kinda missed lunch today, Guy," JP said, "and I was hoping a friendly person would show up to help me celebrate."

"He's leaving us," Jennifer said. JP still wasn't sure if she was actually mad or simply playing the part. "Your best customer is leaving you."

"It's only for a few months. I'll be back by spring."

"Bummer," Guy said while exchanging the pizza for payment and a nice tip. "What about Bubba? Will he be going, too?"

"Yes, JP, did you think about Bubba?"

"Where I'm going, he can't follow. What I've got to do, he can't be any part of," JP said.

"Really?" Jennifer spurted out. "You choose a time like this to misquote 'Casablanca'?"

"I did not misquote it; I paraphrased it. Would you kindly take the pizza or Bubba, please? Guy, I'm going to work in Antarctica for a few months, but it's temporary. You can bet you'll be one of my first calls when I return."

"Antarctica, huh? That's cool."

"So they say, Guy; so they say."

SEPTEMBER 14, 5:57 P.M.

"Seriously, JP, I'm all kinds of happy for you," Jennifer said as she opened the pizza. "I mean, I don't know much about Antarctica, but it's got to be an interesting experience. What I don't understand is why you kept it a secret until now?"

"The only secret I kept was the fact I applied and, I guess, the fact I was chosen as an alternate. Remember that phone call this morning from the 720 area code? That's when I heard they wanted me."

Jennifer's stare indicated the answer wasn't good enough.

"OK, I could have told everyone when I applied back in May, but it was such long odds and it raises so many questions, I decided to keep it between Stanley and me. I had to get his promise there would be a job here when I returned.

"Once I was offered the standby position, I had to go through an unbelievable set of physical exams, including having my wisdom teeth removed. You don't know how many doctor visits I made this summer. I didn't want to drag my friends through all of that."

"And what about Bubba?"

"Even before I adopted Bubba, Andrea said she would keep him if I needed help."

"Andrea Munoz? Our secretary?"

"Yeah, but four to five months might be more than I should ask or more than she could handle, so I was kinda hoping you would volunteer to help her. You and Bubba get along so great."

"I'd have been offended had you not asked. If Andrea's still interested, I'm sure we could work out a joint custody arrangement. Otherwise, he can stay with me, can't you, fella?"

The ferret always seemed to know when he was the subject of conversation and poked his head out of a box right on cue, only to dart out of the room when they started laughing.

SEPTEMBER 15, 8:45 A.M.

"Short-timer alert," yelled city reporter Archie Hanning as JP entered the temporary news room carrying an empty cardboard box. A boo sounded from the back and JP shook his head, unable to hide a bit of a grin.

"I'm certainly feeling the love now," he said, but was cut off by Pat Baird.

"JP, hon, I was just suggesting to everyone that we should all try to get together for lunch here to give you a chance to tell us your side of the story and maybe field questions instead of you having to go through it all several times."

"There is a reason this lady holds the title Queen of the News Room," JP said loud enough for all to hear. "I brought my lunch, so I'm good to go. I should be back here by 11:30; any time after that is great. Right now, though, I have a meeting with a guy at the SCAB."

SEPTEMBER 15, 9:20 A.M.

"The SCAB," JP said out loud while shaking his head as he pulled his pickup into the small parking lot at State College-Oldport. The nickname originated at State College's main campus, whose students referred to the Oldport campus as State College At the Beach.

It currently looked the part of a healing wound as most buildings suffered considerable damage from Hurricane Clarice. State College sent a team down to patch up things well enough to get by, but it was obvious the small branch wasn't at the top of the repair list because the inland main campus had widespread, if not as severe, damage itself.

JP headed toward the largest building, but a voice stopped him as he reached for the door.

"Mr. Weiscarver, I hoped to intercept you." JP immediately recognized the New England accent of Marcellus Stapler.

"Dr. Stapler, I so appreciate you seeing me on such short notice."

"Don't be silly. You're about to join the league of Antarctic explorers; I owe it to you to help anyway I can."

"Especially since you're responsible for me considering it in the first place."

"A designation that thrills me, JP. Why don't we grab a bench outside? My office hasn't been air-conditioned since the storm. So, what are your top questions? I say 'top' because I know there are plenty."

JP thought about it just a second, his right hand massaging his chin as if powering the process.

"Well, the information from USAP seemed thorough about what to take."

"One suggestion. I wasn't on station much since most of my time was on the traverse and in field camp, but I did find the buildings were well heated. What I'm saying is, pack warm but throw in a couple of T-shirts as well. I think you'll be surprised."

"I understand there's a gym where I can shoot a few hoops. What else occupies my down time?"

"First of all, they help by making sure you work long hours."

"Six days a week, nine hours a day," JP affirmed. "But I often approach that here."

"Since you simply show up for meals and eat, that doesn't take up much time. The only cleaning you do is your room and maybe your workplace. So, you're right, there's still plenty of free time. It seems like even more because the sun shines all of the time. One of my first days there, in late November, Shane Peltzer and I took a hike on what they call Hut Point Ridge Trail. We lost track of time and didn't get back until 2 a.m., but the sun was still shining bright, as it was when I had to get out of bed at 6:30."

"Were you and Peltzer close?"

"I don't think anyone was close to him," Stapler said after brief consideration. "Most teams have their odd member and he was ours. He was a support assistant, more technician than scientist, and didn't really fit in. That's not reason enough to not like him, mind you. For example, everyone got along great with support lead Josh Smith, but Shane was just an odd duck. Back to your questions."

JP took the hint and glanced down at his checklist.

"I'll admit I'm a little concerned about having a roommate."

"Yes, that's a big one for many people. I roomed with one of my partners, of course, so that relieved some of the anxiety. The rooms I saw were tiny with a bunk bed or two and what I'd call wardrobes – metal drawers below a hanging rack for clothes. I think most have a desk, chairs, something like that."

After they talked more than half an hour, JP noticed Stapler fidgeting with his watch and deduced it was time to wrap things up.

"One last thing, when will your team be down?"

"Our deployment date is Nov. 4. Instead of an overland traverse to get to our research site like we did last year, we'll be able to fly in by LC-130 aircraft, the ones with snow skis. Everything is simpler this year since we're primarily gathering data from equipment we left in place last year. Well, not that simple but indeed easier. It will take several weeks to then reposition the equipment some 10 kilometers and get everything up and running again."

"Why the traverse last year? From what I've read about the LC-130, it can carry just about anything."

"True, in fact they will carry out our equipment next year. We built our grant proposal around delivering the project by traverse because we felt like that enhanced its acceptability. Getting National Science Foundation grants can be pretty competitive, so we structured the testing of another grantee's new polar transportation equipment into our proposal, kind of like giving the NSF two projects in one. Additionally, the aircraft are especially busy earlier in the season, which was when we had to go last year, so the strategy made that more appealing, too."

"Have you heard if there will be further efforts to recover Shane Peltzer's body?"

"That appears unlikely. A search and rescue team responded to our camp after Shane wandered off. We searched for two days without finding any trace. We're left to presume he either fell into a crevasse or deliberately walked off to his death, a theory I find difficult to accept. Some have said he could have simply gotten lost, freaked out and started acting crazy. In that scenario, there's no way to guess what he would have done. Regardless, without additional evidence, they've indicated it's not prudent to attempt further searches."

SEPTEMBER 15, 10:11 A.M.

JP found his mind swirling as he headed back to the temporary Odds and Ends news room.

Last night, he talked to his landlords, Wes and Donna Simpson, and they were totally cooperative, agreeing to keep an eye on the house while he was gone. He still needed to contact utilities and arrange to have them cut off.

"My cell phone," he said out loud. "I can't use a cell phone in Antarctica."

His thoughts went quiet again as he decided to see if he could suspend his contract; he'd heard of that somewhere before.

He had a good idea of what clothes and personal effects would go with him. Some were already sacked up, others on a list. Any shopping would be done at his parents, where he planned to spend three or four days. The idea of shopping for cold weather clothing in a southern city nearly destroyed by a hurricane was laughable.

"I need to let my folks know I'm coming," he said, making himself concentrate on traffic as he neared downtown. "I think I'll try to wait until I'm there before I tell them what's happening. Wonder how Momma's going to take it?"

As JP approached the police station, he noticed Jennifer's green car parked at the curb and he made an instant decision to pull into a neighboring spot.

"I can't leave without telling Tad goodbye."

SEPTEMBER 15, 10:22 A.M.

"Hey, Sarge, what's shaking in the world of thick coffee and thicker doughnuts?" JP blurted out as he entered the small office of Oldport Police Department's PIO – public information officer – Sergeant Tad Bellew.

Bellew kept his attention focused on the newspaper's cops reporter sitting across the desk from him. "Do you think, Miss O'Hanlon, your co-worker will ever tire of that opening line?"

"Former co-worker," Jennifer corrected.

"True, true," Bellew said while JP helped himself to a cup of the policeman's near-famous coffee. "I understand we're no longer far enough south for him, that he's willing to go all the way to the South Pole just to get away from us."

"Not the South Pole, Tad ... well, I do hope to get to go there ... but I'll be working primarily in McMurdo Station. And, don't take it personally. Someone has to go and, what the heck, maybe I can help broaden y'all's world view a bit."

"So, you're doing it for us," Bellew said, finally addressing JP directly. "That's, uh, that's downright generous of you. When are you leaving?"

"Maybe tomorrow, if everything falls together, the next day for sure. I'm driving to my parents to do some final shopping and leave my pickup. The program is securing flights for me from there to Denver and then on to New Zealand."

"New Zealand?"

"That's the jumping off point for almost all of the U.S. participants. Military aircraft fly from Christchurch to McMurdo."

"What does your mother think about all of this?" Jennifer asked.

"Oh, she loves the idea; she and Dad both are really excited for me," JP answered. He then gave a blank stare at the ceiling. "At least, I'm sure they will be as soon as I tell them about it."

SEPTEMBER 15, 10:58 A.M.

"Hello, Momma. How are you and Daddy doing?

"No, no, I'm great. Really. I'm driving right now, but I'm headed to the office. Yes, ma'am, I'm always careful.

"Listen, would y'all mind if I popped up there to visit you for two or three days? I'll leave tomorrow, I think, but maybe the next day. I'll call and let you know when to expect me.

"Yes, everything is fine. It's great, actually. No, I didn't lose my job, but I do have some big news. Of course I'm not getting married. I'd at least let you know I had a girlfriend first.

"Yes, Momma, I am being evasive. Because I'd rather tell both of you in person. Well, that will give the two of you something to speculate on over dinner tonight. I promise there is no bad news."

JP was parked by the time he hung up and realized Jennifer was standing outside his open door.

"So, Momma Weiscarver still doesn't know?"

"Don't judge, O'Hanlon. Once I tell her, there will be a thousand points of worry I'll have to address, something done much more effectively in person and with Dad's assistance. She thought I was going to the ends of the earth when I moved south to the coast."

SEPTEMBER 15, 1:14 P.M.

Tying up loose ends at the office took less time than JP anticipated.

The "bon voyage" meeting went smoothly. He was able to answer most of the questions and felt as if he had raised the level of Antarctic awareness just a little.

More disturbing than anything else, it seemed, was the realization they could not just pick up the phone and call him.

"I'll be by my e-mail much of the time," he told them, "but keep in mind we'll be like 18 or 19 hours ahead of you. When you come to work in the morning, I may just be going to bed. You cannot call me, but I can call out if there's an open line. I'll have to pay long-distance charges from Denver, through which the satellite is linked."

Yeah, he thought, that's going to be the scariest part for Momma. Good thing I got to practice with the guys at work.

His mind was swimming so that he almost forgot to stop at Oldport Utilities to arrange cutting off his services.

SEPTEMBER 15, 6:09 P.M.

JP was busy patting himself on the back while Bubba grabbed yet another nap in the corner of the sofa.

The ferret half-opened an eye when his human started talking out loud again.

"I believe that's it. I never thought I could get my belongings pared down to one large bag. Well, Bubba, looks like we're both packed now," he said while reaching for the ferret.

Before he got there, the doorbell rang and Bubba raced to the front room.

"And just in the nick of time," JP said as he finally scooped up his four-legged friend and answered the door, where he found Jennifer O'Hanlon and Andrea Munoz. As they entered, fawning over Bubba, JP saw his neighbor, Jason Nash, arrive home. He quickly handed over the center of attention and excused himself.

"Hey, Jason," he yelled out before his neighbor reached the door. They visited a moment, mainly about Jason's wait for repairs to his hurricane-damaged home, before JP filled him in on his situation.

"I just wanted you to know what was going on and to give you the phone number for my landlords. They will keep an eye on things, but I'd appreciate you alerting them if you see something strange. Finally, and this might be the most important part, I have a refrigerator almost full of food that I need to get rid of."

By the time JP returned home, Jennifer and Andrea had organized Bubba's cage, sleeping pad, bowls and bags of food.

"We're ready," Jennifer said. "I will take Bubba first, but we'll switch out every week or so, depending on our schedules."

"So soon?" JP asked.

"We're ripping off the bandage," Andrea replied with an authoritative air. "We also found your instructions. I'm sure they will be helpful."

"Just make sure he gets plenty of interaction. Ferrets are social critters and he can become depressed if he's alone too much."

"Uh, yes, I believe that's No. 14 on your list," Jennifer said, referring to the printout. "Right after 'Change his drinking water daily.'"

"OK, OK, point taken. I'm sure you're both better prepared than I was when Bubba moved in here. Yeah, y'all go on, I have a lot to do anyway," JP said, releasing a long, loud sigh.

"He's almost cute when he mopes," Andrea said to Jennifer.

"Almost."

SEPTEMBER 16, 5:24 A.M.

It was early, but JP knew he was awake for the day. Still, he continued to lie in bed, thoughts racing through his mind.

He found actual relief in the idea of leaving behind the daily newspaper grind in favor of more in-depth work. At least, that's how he perceived his new job to be, trying to explain scientific research to a lay readership.

That idea, though, was a bit intimidating in itself. He liked to think that, given good sources, he could clearly report anything, but was he really capable of working with what must be the world's leading minds in things like glaciology and cosmology?

After all, he'd always thought of himself as a generalist, possessing just enough knowledge about a broad spectrum of topics to be able to ask good questions and then follow the answers to a reasonable degree.

He quickly shook off the concerns and rolled out of bed.

"Enough of that," he said to his mirror. "I can do this and do it well. Antarctica, here I come."

SEPTEMBER 16, 10:33 A.M.

Naturally, it took longer than JP hoped to finish packing his truck for the drive home, but he had built extra time into his schedule. He planned three short days of driving with two stops en route to visit with college buddies. Between the pressures of hurricane recovery and a new job in a remote location, he decided a mini-vacation would be wise.

He was tempted to swing by the temporary newspaper office again, but dismissed the thought. Goodbyes were said and another visit would only disrupt their work again. As he pointed his pickup north, he was struck with another thought.

"Church! In all my rush, I didn't inform anyone at church that I'd be gone."

He was glad to see the Rev. Ann Dickenson's car in her usual parking spot as he pulled into the lot and was a little surprised to find her at her desk. It seemed like she was always busying around taking care of something and he had wondered how she found time to write a sermon every week.

"Pastor Ann, you got a minute?" he asked at the door to get her attention. He was already entering, though, because he knew the answer to the question.

In short order, they exchanged pleasantries and he told her of his looming adventure.

"Antarctica, huh?" she let the words slip out as if a thought. Then she looked more squarely at JP and nodded her encouragement. "I understand it gets pretty chilly up there."

"Down there," JP gently corrected, "and that's what I hear, too."

"Yes, down there; Antarctica's the South Pole and the Arctic is the North Pole. Well, four months is a long time, JP. We'll miss you, but you know we'll be here when you come back."

"Indeed, I do. If Hurricane Clarice couldn't budge this church, I trust it will stand up to my absence. By the way, they do have both Protestant and Roman Catholic chaplains on the Ice during the summer season and there's even a chapel where they hold weekly services, so I'll be able to stay in touch, too."

"I'm not worried about you," she said and shared one of her warm smiles. "You have a good head on your shoulders. Here, take a couple of my cards and give one to your chaplain and tell him to call me if he needs help understanding you."

With a laugh, he took the cards and told her he would consider doing that.

With a prayer for safe adventures, JP left Pastor Ann's

office feeling a little bit better about his plans and the world in general. It was a good way to put Oldport into his rearview mirror as he turned north again.

SEPTEMBER 18, 3:31 P.M.

The drive home, while long, was relaxing, but JP was glad to see the water tower as he approached town.

During his more than five years in Oldport, he had fallen in love with the sometimes quirky coastal life. He knew it wasn't likely he would be there forever, but it was possible. He considered, as he drove old, familiar streets, that he might even hang around and eventually be city editor in Oldport, become a combination of Pat Baird and Stanley Hopper.

His attention turned to a popular teenage hangout, the spot where some girl ... her name evaded him ... turned down his request to "go steady." This would always be his hometown, he thought, but it seemed near impossible he would ever live here again.

"I wouldn't trade anything for my experiences here," he said to no one, "but there are other places I'm meant to be."

His father wouldn't be home for a couple of hours and JP decided that was too much time to be with his mother and not tell her his plans, so he made a course correction for a city park.

Five minutes later, he was sitting at a picnic table, allowing his driving muscles to relax and his brain to safely wander.

His first thoughts were recalling how much more quickly fall came here than in Oldport. It was noticeably cooler and some leaves were turning.

Speaking of cooler, he checked a weather app on his cell phone and saw it was minus 18 degrees Fahrenheit in McMurdo Station.

He let his mind roam through various ideas of what life

will be like for the next four or five months. His musings never got too far, he soon realized, because he just did not know enough about what lay before him to formulate significant story lines.

"It's like trying to write a news story without interviewing the subject or witnessing the event," he mumbled to himself. "Maybe that's why I want to do this, so I know for myself what it is like."

SEPTEMBER 18, 5:12 P.M.

As JP turned into the driveway of the home of Jay and Penelope Weiscarver, he saw his mother opening the front door for his father. She then almost pushed Jay off the porch before he realized she had spotted their son and headed to meet him.

Both were at his side by the time he opened the door. Hugs and hellos gave way to them standing there, Penelope's attention locked on the bags, much more than JP usually visited with.

"Did you bring dirty laundry?" she asked.

"No, Momma," JP started. "Well, actually, I did bring some because I didn't want to leave any dirty clothes behind, but the reason for the extra baggage is the big news I have for you."

He managed to delay the discussion until his bags were in the house and his mother motioned for them to sit around the dining table.

The move was not lost on her son. She was not convinced his news wasn't bad. Happy and friendly visits took place in the den. Serious conversation happened over the dining table. He cast a glance at his dad, who slightly arched an eyebrow while pulling out a chair for his wife.

"First, let me apologize for allowing this to become so dramatic," JP said. "I should have just told you over the phone, but, then again, I was afraid you'd be overcome with questions and concerns and I wouldn't be handy to answer them. So ..."

This was not going the way he had planned.

"I've taken a job working in Antarctica."

"You're moving to the North Pole?" his mother blurted out.

"No, the South Pole, well, down toward the South Pole..."

"South Pole? That's even farther. We'll never see you."

Was that a sob, JP wondered.

"And I'm not moving; it's temporary, less than five months. It's like a special assignment. Dad, do you understand?" he asked, looking for help.

"I think so, son. You've taken a five-month job and then you'll be home to get a real job again."

Oh, wow, JP thought, I didn't expect this to be so difficult.

"I still have my job in Oldport. They're allowing me a leave of absence and they're holding my job for me. I won't be unemployed. I'll just get to do something different for a while and go someplace most people never get to."

It occurred to JP he was pushing too hard. He forgot to allow his mother processing time. She was reasonable enough, but she had a tendency to begin dealing with a problem with a knee-jerk reaction. He sat quietly, awaiting the questions he knew would come.

Once they did, both of his parents were better tuned in to what he had to say. His father even started taking notes. They discussed the travel schedule, his work on the Ice and the fact he still had a job when he returned, what he would eat, Thanksgiving and Christmas, safety, communication and clothing.

"So, we need to go shopping," Penelope said. She saw JP smile. "Oh, you don't need me to help you buy clothes," she added.

"No, Momma, I've been buying my own clothes for a decade now. But, if you have time tomorrow, I think it could be fun if we went together."

SEPTEMBER 22, 6:34 P.M.

Jennifer O'Hanlon answered on the second ring.

"Hey, JP, I wondered when you'd find time to check in."

"I've actually stayed pretty busy. I was afraid these five days would drag, but it's been a fun time. How's Bubba?"

"He's great, doesn't miss you one bit. So, did you ever tell Momma Weiscarver you're going to Antarctica or are you just going to send her a postcard?"

"Are you kidding? She wouldn't let me into the house until I shared my secret. It was a rough start, but she rebounded quickly and soon got wrapped up in the excitement. We've had a lot of fun. It's kind of like she's finally released me to be an adult in addition to being a son."

"Yeah, I know what you mean; I'm still waiting for that. Oh, Lydia came into the office today."

"And how is Ms. Murray?"

"Recovering nicely and planning on being back at work by mid-October. She was simultaneously saddened and thrilled by your news. She didn't say so, but I think she was disappointed not to see you before you left."

"I came close to going by, but, I don't know, it just seemed awkward. I finally decided to call her after I get settled in on the Ice."

There was a brief pause before Jennifer again picked up the conversation.

"So, are you ready? You go to Denver tomorrow, right?"

"Yeah, my folks are driving me to the little regional airport nearby. Flight leaves at 9:20 a.m. Am I ready? I hope so. I bought two soft-sided bags for my stuff. My mother calls them body bags. They're loaded with just about everything except my toothbrush. I've even laid out the clothes I'll wear on the flight, including slip-on shoes to ease through security. I don't think there's another thing I could do to be better prepared."

"Well, I put you on speaker during that story and there's a critter in my lap soaking up every word. Maybe the last thing you need to do is say, 'Good night, Bubba.'"

"Good night, Bubba. I miss you, buddy."

"What's that, Bubba? Oh, he said, 'Safe travels.' And that's from both of us."

SEPTEMBER 23, 8:47 A.M.

JP's parents chose to walk him into the airport and hung around to make sure there had been no changes to his flight. The three of them waved their goodbyes once he passed the security checkpoint and he found a seat near his gate.

By now, the plane had disgorged passengers from its previous shuttle run. While awaiting the call to seat passengers toward the rear of the plane, JP's mind was flying all over the map.

He'd be in Denver in a few hours after a brief layover in Chicago. His employer arranged a shuttle van to take him to his hotel, which would provide a ride tomorrow morning to offices of the U.S. Antarctic Program.

There would undoubtedly be more paperwork, but the emphasis for the first few days was meeting the rest of the journalism team and planning their summer on Ice.

JP grinned, thinking about the number of times the past nine days he had said, "Of course, it will be summer down there since it's in the Southern Hemisphere."

"Wow," he said under his breath.

"I beg your pardon," said a woman two chairs down.

"I'm going to Antarctica. Where are you headed?"

SEPTEMBER 23, 4:11 P.M.

23

Excited as he was beginning the trip, JP was dragging by the time he reached Denver.

The flights, connections and baggage all went smoothly. He lugged everything to the appropriate level of the appropriate terminal at the sprawling Denver International Airport and found a series of lanes with commuter shuttles zipping in and out.

Taking a deep breath, the self-described small town boy remembered to check the information in his pocket, which said he was to go to Island 3 and look for the name of his shuttle. Easy enough, he thought two minutes later as he placed his bags under the correct sign and stretched his once-athletic frame by slowly touching his toes.

After waiting a few minutes, he was approached by a fast-talking driver from a neighboring station asking if he was at the right place.

"I think so," JP said, producing his information, at which the driver cast a glance and started nodding his head.

"Yes, yes, he left just before you got here. He won't be back for a long time."

While talking, he was pressing familiar buttons on his cell phone and his conversation turned from JP to the other driver, this time in a language the reporter could not identify.

The discussion seemed heated at times, or maybe that was a cultural thing, JP thought, but the driver suddenly gave an obvious farewell and redirected his attention.

"I will take you to your hotel."

"You don't understand," he said, "my ride was prepaid."

"I know, I know my friend. Don't you worry. I take you and he pay me. Don't you worry, we do this all the time. We come from the same country. Most of us here come from the same country and we all help each other."

JP shrugged his agreement, not knowing what else to do, and the driver added, "I have my own rider but his hotel is between here and yours, so I drop him off first, OK?"

His new fare agreed and asked the driver his name.

"My America friends, they call me 'Bubba.'"

JP laughed and handed over his last bag. "OK, Bubba, I feel better already."

SEPTEMBER 24, 8:55 A.M.

The hotel courtesy shuttle dropped off JP in front of a large glass-fronted building with maybe a dozen steps leading up to the front door.

Once he was buzzed in, a woman checked his identification, had him sign in and issued him a temporary access card. As he was about to ask her what happened next, he heard someone call his name.

"JP, welcome to the U.S. Antarctic Program. I'm Sally Hutchens."

"It will seem as if we're throwing a lot at you this week," Sally said as she escorted JP up a stairway that featured a huge map of the frozen continent, "and that's because we will be throwing a lot at you, but don't become overwhelmed. Both of your teammates on the Ice were there last year and we will all have your back until you're up and running. We know you're getting tossed into the mix late, but the only thing you can do wrong right now is to not ask questions or request help."

Inside a cubbyhole office, she introduced JP to the assistant manager, Ruthann Lesley, who promptly hopped up and gave him a welcome hug.

"You're the person who fielded all my e-mail and phone questions," JP said, knowing already that he would get along with the folks here.

"We are so tickled you could join us on such short notice," Ruthann said. "I told Sal once I talked to you on the phone that you are a perfect cog for our little machine."

"She did and Ruthann is always right. Come on. Your Ice partners are in a meeting room working out the details of your summer budget.

As Sal and JP entered the room, two faces simultaneously looked up from a table with several sheets of paper lined up. The two then looked at each other and yelled, "Fingie!"

"Folks, meet JP Weiscarver. JP, our lead journalist here is Simon Burlle, who is returning for his third summer with The Antarctic Sun. And this is the former newbie, Alexia Jones."

After a couple of minutes, Sal excused herself and the three new teammates spent another 30 minutes getting to know one another and answering JP's questions.

"You shouted 'fingie' when I came in," JP said, noticing the two again exchanged grins. "OK, 'fess up."

"It's the pronunciation of the acronym FNGI," Simon volunteered.

"That stands for New Guy on Ice," finished Alexia. "I don't remember what the F stands for."

"Understood," JP said, exchanging high-fives with his new partners.

SEPTEMBER 28, 11:32 A.M.

JP sat on a retaining wall outside the USAP office's side door waiting for the other four members of the team to join him for lunch. Reflecting on the past five days, they seemed in some ways to have flown by and in others to have lasted a month.

With input from an assortment of scientists and program officials, the three-person Ice team pounded out a week-by-week schedule of story ideas. Simon stressed that while they would attempt to stay as close to the schedule as they could, many changes will happen.

The key is to have several stories in some phase of development at one time. One story that has to slide back because a scientist rescheduled could be replaced by another that was almost ready to wrap up.

Many of the stories assigned JP did not make much sense to him. He spent time each evening reviewing science planning summaries. An SPS gave key information about a science project, including a brief description that usually made it easier to understand. It also listed the principal investigator (PI), participating institutions and the various members who would deploy to the Ice.

Simon made it a point to assign JP the story on the atmospheric study which involved the Oldport professor, Marcellus Stapler. He also gave him an assignment that should net a trip to the South Pole.

JP was pleased he would write several stories about life on the Ice, that they would not all be solely about scientific research.

In addition to all of the work the journalism team had achieved during the week, JP had gotten to know several others who were bound for the Ice to perform a wide assortment of jobs. Riding the shuttle back and forth between headquarters and the hotel, he had buddied up with a fresh college graduate who would work "shoveling snow, or whatever else they tell me" and with a registered nurse who came out of retirement to work at the bottom of the world.

Relaxing in the warm sun on this cool autumn day, JP thought about the hot weather that still had its grip on Oldport. He closed his eyes and pictured the expansive, open beach and the waters of the Gulf of Mexico, contrasting it with the views he had here of the Rocky Mountains.

"That's nothing," he said to himself. "Next stop, New Zealand."

2 TO THE ICE

JP often talked of his love of travel and ambitions to see the world, but the fact he had never gotten too far from home really sank in as he watched for his two checked bags to find their way onto the carousel at Christchurch International Airport.

The vast majority of the past 27 hours had been on airplanes, flying from Denver to Los Angeles to Auckland to here.

Christchurch is the nearest major airport to McMurdo Station and is also the New Zealand base of operations for the U.S. Antarctic Program. Almost all Americans on the Ice journey through Christchurch, or Cheech, as many called it.

During the flights, JP chalked up firsts by crossing the International Date Line, by venturing into the Southern Hemisphere and by spending all night on a plane.

Finally, with bags in hand, he met greeters from the program who handed him an envelope with his room assignment and two days of spending money in Kiwi dollars. He grabbed the next to last available seat on a shuttle van that towed a small cargo trailer to handle the large amount of baggage.

He gave the driver the name of his assigned backpacker on Gloucester Street. Reservations were made by the Antarctic Program after getting JP's input on his desired type of lodging – meaning how much he wanted to spend.

A backpacker inn, to the best of JP's understanding, was a step above a hostel. He would have his own Spartan room with a shared bath down the hall. He would pay for lodging and his meals out of the per diem allowed by the program.

En route, he discovered one of his new friends, a dining room attendant from Alaska, was also in the van and staying in the same place, so they made plans to roam Christchurch and find dinner together.

"Spartan, indeed," JP said as he entered the room, which might have been as large as a jail cell. There was a bunk bed, a nightstand and one chair. He stacked his large bags in the corner and plopped his carry-on atop the lower bed to determine what clothes he wanted to spread out on the top bed since there were no hangers.

Soon, he searched for the rest room and balked when there was no "men" or "women" designation. Entering, he learned why. Men and women shared the same rest room facilities, as well as the same showers. Each toilet and shower had locks to provide privacy.

"Bubba," he whispered to his faraway ferret, "I have a feeling we're not in Oldport anymore."

OCTOBER 1, 8:12 P.M.

After roaming around Christchurch for nearly an hour, JP and Richard Mozell ended up in an Indian restaurant and spent much too long exploring the menu and sampling dishes.

Richard, who was probably 10 years JP's senior, wasn't originally from Alaska but ended up calling it home after he bailed out of the corporate world in search of adventure.

"I keep busy during the tourist months working with some outfitter or as a fishing guide, maybe as a dishwasher or in housekeeping at a hotel, just about anything that doesn't require too much paperwork, too many bosses and absolutely no profit and loss statements," he said in explaining his current life choice.

"What about during the winter?" JP asked.

"Let's see; I've been in Alaska for seven years now and have spent only one winter there, the first one. I'm originally from Arizona and, while I don't really care for the hot summers there anymore, I'm still not up to handling a central Alaskan winter. So, I've worked in a couple of parks, spent one season cleaning toilets for a theme park in Florida, another tending cattle on a small ranch in southern Texas. Now I'll work as a dining room attendant in McMurdo. I'm not exactly sure what that entails, but a summer on the Ice is bound to be warmer than a winter in Alaska."

"Sounds like you have it all figured out."

"Oh, I hope not," Richard said. "Once you get it all figured out, it's bound to get boring."

OCTOBER 2, 1:49 P.M.

JP found it easy to spend all morning wandering the streets, shops and tourist sites of Christchurch, but returned to his room in plenty of time to meet a shuttle van that was to pick him up at 2 p.m. Walking out the front door about 10 minutes early, he saw the van pull up.

"Mozell and Weiscarver," the driver called out as he exited the right side of the vehicle, something JP was not used to seeing. Waving at the driver, JP produced a couple of New Zealand's colorful bills to pay for the ride back to the airport area. He then pointed out Richard, who was just leaving the building.

Slipping into the front seat alongside the driver, JP was greeted by calls from Simon Burlle and Alexia Jones, his journalism partners who were staying in a hotel a couple of blocks away.

"Are you ready for your fitting?" Simon asked.

"Probably not, but that's why I have several of my new best friends along for the ride," JP said, extending a fist over the back of the car seat to get a fist bump from Richard.

OCTOBER 2, 2:36 P.M.

Their destination was named, simply and appropriately enough, the Clothing Distribution Center. Like most things in the program, it was reduced to an acronym and even the shuttle drivers all referred to it as the CDC.

Once inside and divided with the men going to the left and women to the right, JP found two orange bags with his name on them. His chore for the next hour or so was trying on all of the clothing in the bags, checking to make sure everything fit and seemed to be in good shape. There were some things that were totally new to him.

"What do you call this?" he asked Simon while pulling what he would have called a ninja mask over his head.

"A balaclava and at least you figured out how to wear it. That or a knit hat is one of the items of clothing you're required to have on during flights. Have you tried on the wind pants yet?"

"Are those the overall-looking contraptions? No, I started to and put them back for now."

Someone JP didn't know laughed at that.

"Yeah, they're often confusing, but we'll figure it out," Simon said.

Extreme Cold Weather gear – or ECW – was the collective term for the specially designed clothing which could cover every inch of his body.

There was an assortment of gloves, from lightweight glove liners to heavy, furry mittens. There was even an Elmer Fudd hat with ear flaps. Goggles shielded the eyes while neck and face protection was enhanced by a neck gaiter.

Headlining the ECW were two iconic items he had seen in many of the photos – bunny boots and Big Red.

The bulbous white boots had thick layers of insulation and a valve that had to be opened while airborne. They were required wear for any flights.

Big Red, also required on flights, was the nickname for the heavy parka issued each participant. When JP tried on his, he immediately felt it was capable of keeping him warm. Another level of disbelief was lifted when he looked in a mirror and saw his face sticking out of the furry lining of the coat's hood. On the chest was a name tag, "J.P. Weiscarver."

"Oh, well, they got close," JP said.

"Don't admire yourself too long," Simon said. "We have to be back in a little over 12 hours to put everything on for real."

OCTOBER 2, 7:54 P.M.

Before turning in early, JP visited an Internet cafe down the street and spent the better part of an hour sending and reading e-mails. Finally, he got around to writing the one he had put off.

"Let's see," he mumbled while stroking his chin. "It's 8:45 p.m. here and we're 18 hours ahead of home. Add six hours and subtract a day, so it's 2:45 a.m. today. Good, she won't be online now. What to say? Come on, you're a writer. Write."

His fingers hovered for a few seconds but then took over.

"Lydia, greetings from the other side of the world. New Zealand is entering spring now and Christchurch is alive with flowers; it's a beautiful place. We're 18 hours ahead of you, so I'm about to go back to my room and get some sleep before getting up at 3 a.m. to start the trip to Antarctica.

"Listen, Lydia, I've been troubled by the fact I didn't get by to see you and your mom before leaving. It all happened so quickly and I had so much to take care of, but that's not really an excuse. I'm sorry I didn't drop in.

"The real reason I hesitated, I suppose, was because I don't want to get in the way of where your career is headed. You've leaned on me a bit getting started and that's perfect execution on your part, considering how you had to work your way into newspapers, learning the ropes as you go.

"I've always said you have what it takes, but you're so much better equipped than I realized. You proved it over and over during the hurricane coverage. In addition to performing top-notch journalism, you also exceled as a member of the community. Bottom line, I am incredibly proud of you and will always treasure the fact that I was there when you started.

"That's why I didn't come by, I guess. I didn't know how to say that in person ... the curse of being a writer. Good luck as you get back to work at the Odds and Ends and please do not totally take over my job before I return in February."

OCTOBER 3, 3:53 A.M.

The shuttle experience repeated itself, this time in the darkness of early spring night. The other difference was the fact JP carried all of his belongings with him.

A small covered trailer behind the van became home for the bags while JP popped into the back seat.

"A little quieter today," he remarked while the others made room for him.

"Going to be a long day," Simon mumbled.

"I'm just hoping we don't get a boomerang. The weather was iffy yesterday," said someone JP did not know.

"It's always iffy this time of year," Simon said.

"What's a boomerang?" asked Richard, who was already settled into a middle seat.

The reporter fielded the question.

"It's when a flight leaves for the Ice but has to turn around and come back because of deteriorating weather conditions. That's why you were told to pack your carry-on for an overnight stay. In the case of a boomerang, they'll keep our luggage on pallets so they'll be ready to go when the weather is cooperating."

"That would take a lot of the fun out of getting up at this hour," Richard said.

Once at the CDC, JP was busy changing into his ECW as required for the flight, well aware that the reason for the rule was to be better prepared for a disaster. If the aircraft went down in the middle of nowhere, survivors would presumably at least have gear nearby to help them not freeze to death anytime soon.

With his bags then entrusted to the loadmaster, JP lugged his carry-on and Big Red to a meeting room.

"I thought we were through with the training," he whispered to Alexia Jones.

"We're never through with training. The first thing we'll do on the Ice is have another meeting and be reminded of what we must and must not do."

"I had a high school coach who said you had to hear something six times to remember it."

"Well, due to inflation, that's now 28 times."

OCTOBER 3, 6:55 A.M.

Numbed by a short sleep followed by a monotone safety meeting, JP came to when he exited the CDC into a crisp New Zealand spring sunrise.

Even though the CDC is located next to Christchurch International Airport, a bus was employed to transport the passengers onto the apron to the waiting Air Force C-17 cargo plane.

Exiting the bus, each traveler was handed a hefty sack lunch, a pair of disposable ear plugs and then channeled toward the aircraft. JP found it impossible to thoroughly take in everything because it all happened so quickly. These folks have done this too many times, he thought but dismissed the idea that he yell for everyone to stop and enjoy the moment. That would definitely be a FNGI mistake. The thought was interrupted when an airman handed him a set of disposable earplugs.

The interior of the plane featured rows of passenger seats, the apparent comfort and roominess of each would leave one welcoming a cramped commercial flight. JP quickly decided to grab one of the jump seats that lined the cabin. There, at least, he could stretch out his legs a bit.

Following more instruction and considerable waiting, the aircraft taxied to the runway and unceremoniously took flight.

After looking around a bit at his fellow travelers and realizing conversation would be next to impossible due to the roar of the engines, JP pulled a paperback book from an interior pocket of his parka and settled back to read until finding a fitful sleep.

Time crawled when he was awake. He put forth the effort to chat with someone on occasion, ate half of his sack lunch, walked around a bit and stood in line for a chance to use the rest room.

Activity increased in the cabin when word got around that ice was visible below. He glanced at his watch and estimated 90 minutes until arrival.

OCTOBER 3, 1:24 P.M.

Had thoughts of being herded like cattle not crossed

JP's mind in Christchurch, they would have once he deplaned on the sea ice runway at McMurdo Station.

It was somewhat windy and the cold caused him to pull the parka around his face as he walked down the steps. Someone was at the bottom reminding him to take care on the ice and pointing him toward ground transportation.

Communication was still difficult above the roar of the engines and the additional noise of the wind and it was then he noticed a loose line of red parka-clad people, many with their arms outstretched, forming a human barricade to keep him from wandering toward the engines.

Once the line spread out, he paused to look around and noticed whiffs of smoke coming from the distant Mount Erebus, the world's southernmost active volcano, which sits some 25 miles from McMurdo. JP thought to extract his camera and snap his first Antarctic photo just before being encouraged to keep moving.

"Moo," he said without getting comment.

He ended up boarding a vehicle already known to him as Ivan the Terra Bus. Sitting atop six huge, balloon-like tires, the all-wheel-drive bus was a popular fixture at McMurdo and was used for transporting personnel. One more photo and he found himself aboard and soon heading to the nearby station.

Watching as well as he could from his aisle seat, JP saw any number of portable buildings on skids lining the ice road. The scenery turned rocky as the bus left the sea ice and started climbing the volcanic rock upon which McMurdo was built.

After a few turns that robbed him of any orientation, the bus came to a stop and their herder informed them that everyone should move into Building 155 and meet in the galley.

"No, you're not here to eat; that's why they gave you a sack lunch when you left. Find a seat toward the back and wait for a little while."

Others were unloading from different vehicles and

quite a crowd was working its way up the steps of Building 155, pretty much the hub of activities in McMurdo. The steps were heavy metal grates designed to allow ice and snow to pass through and minimize slippery buildup. Falls were one of the station's worst health offenders, he had heard more than once during training.

While climbing the steps he heard the first of several excited squeals as old friends from seasons past were reunited. JP found himself standing and looking around the large entry area when Simon Burlle took hold of his elbow and moved him toward the left.

"This is Highway 1," Simon said as they entered a long, wide hallway. "On the right here is the ship's store. On down the hall are several offices, including housing, recreation, personnel and so on. Here on the left is the coat room, where you'll hang Big Red before entering the galley. No big coats are allowed in there; they knock too much food off tables. Oh, and pay attention where you hang it. They tend to all look alike."

OCTOBER 3, 3:19 P.M.

Mercifully, the meeting was a short re-run of safety rules by station manager Patrick Stiles, who also offered a tour of the station the next morning to whoever was interested.

"I want to do the tour," JP said to Simon as the meeting broke up.

"Good idea. It will give you a quick overview of where things are and a chance to visit with Patrick. You'll certainly get to work with him at one point or another."

"Now, what do I do with this?" he asked, holding up a small brown envelope.

"That's your room assignment. Let me see. Oh, man, you're in 155."

Alexia chimed in at that point: "Sorry, JP, but it's tough being the new guy."

"OK, so what's wrong with 155? That's this building, right? At least I'll be close to meals, right?"

"Right you are, JP," said Simon, "you should stick to the positive. Seriously, the only problem with 155 is that they put four people to a room."

"Ouch. No problem though. Nope, not gonna let it bug me. I didn't come to Antarctica to sit in my room. When do they deliver our bags?"

"They don't. Grab Big Red and we'll head up to MCC; the bags should be ready for pickup now."

"You do that on purpose, don't you?" JP said, tacking on a grin.

"MCC is the Movement Control Center," Alexia said, "Building 140. Basically, people and shipments going in and out are routed through there."

"It also houses the post office, which you'll need later, I'm sure."

OCTOBER 3, 4:07 P.M.

The walk to the MCC was short but cold, windy and a bit of a climb. It was downhill returning to Building 155, but by the time he got to his second-floor room, he was practically dragging one of the body bags.

He found the door open to his room when he got there. Inside, to the right, there were two bunk beds, one on each side of the room, separated by four blue metal lockers, two facing each pair of beds. On the shorter, left end of the room was a love seat, a chair and a TV. Beneath the window directly opposite the door was a small desk.

At the bunk bed to the left, he found Richard Mozell, his Christchurch buddy from Alaska, spreading his belongings across the lower bed in preparation for storing everything into one of the large lockers.

On the other side of the room, an older fellow JP had seen during orientation in Denver had claimed the second bottom bunk, in which he was stretched out relaxing.

"Looks like I'm going up top," the reporter said, picking Richard's side. "You take your time finishing; I'll unpack later."

JP chatted with his other roommate long enough to learn his name was Dan Jenkins, he was a plumber from Maine and was also in his first season in Antarctica. The other top bunk was still unoccupied.

Standing there for a minute while Dan reclined on his bed and Richard unpacked, JP considered living the next four months in a quarter of a dorm room. He quit stroking his chin, shook his head to clear the thought and picked up Big Red.

"I'm going to have a look around. See you guys later."

OCTOBER 3, 5:33 P.M.

It didn't take JP long to get enough of the sub-zero weather, but his quick tour led him by the clinic, the fire station and eventually to the Chalet, the name for the building that housed administrative offices. On its deck, overlooking the sea ice, were a bust of Rear Admiral Richard Evelyn Byrd and flags of the 12 original signatory nations to the Antarctic Treaty – Argentina, Australia, Belgium, Chile, France, Japan, New Zealand, Norway, South Africa, Russia (then the Soviet Union), the United Kingdom and the United States.

The banners flapped loudly in a stiff breeze, which cut JP's viewing time to mere seconds before he turned his back to it and started up the hill to Building 155.

Back in his room, he quickly put away most of his things before heading to the galley for dinner.

The dining room was an organized madhouse. A single line formed at the entry, almost everyone dutifully taking and rubbing on hand sanitizer.

That was one of the major points of training. The Antarctic community was by necessity close. Everyone was packed into dorms and often offices. Rest rooms were shared and each employee and grantee ate out of the same galley.

Germs and viruses could easily pass and affect a large percentage of the population quickly.

Factor in the point hundreds of people were coming together from almost as many places and it's a situation begging for an outbreak.

To combat the threat, people were taught to wash hands frequently, to use hand sanitizer, to control coughs and just practice good hygiene.

JP's hands were dry of the alcohol by the time he reached the stack of dining room trays and plates. As he entered the serving room, there appeared before him a smorgasbord. As promised, there were two meat entrees, a vegetarian entree and a selection of vegetables.

There was also a bowl of fresh fruit, some yummy looking breads and a couple of desserts from which to choose. Finally, diners had several options for drink, including his favorite, iced tea.

People served themselves, taking as little or as much as they wanted. One of the things made clear was one was welcomed to eat all he wanted but was implored to eat all he took. In addition to an effort to save money by not wasting food, the U.S. Antarctic Program had to ship back to the United States all garbage.

Under the Antarctic Treaty, the seventh continent is to be preserved as closely as possible to its natural state. Having a base there is the ultimate camping experience. You pack in what you need and pack out what's left.

The one exception was water. The station used desalinized water from McMurdo Sound and returned that water after extensive sewage treatment.

Entering the split-level dining area, JP spotted Simon and Alexia, both of whom were polishing off a serving of cake.

"Went with the cookies, I see," Simon said as JP took a seat. "Good choice; the cake is a bit dry."

"I'm impressed with the spread," the new guy said. "I think I could get used to this."

"Oh, you'll get used to it, all right," Alexia said. "After a couple of months, it all starts to taste the same."

"Maybe, but it's a winner in my book when all I have to do is walk in, eat and drop off my dirty dishes."

"We swung by your room on the way over," Simon said, "but your roomies said you couldn't wait to get out and play in the snow. Nice guys?"

"One is Richard, an interesting fellow from Alaska I hung out with in Cheech. The other I haven't gotten to know yet. Dan is his name and he's a plumber. We haven't seen No. 4 yet."

"Good luck. Having roommates you enjoy being around makes the experience more enjoyable. If you don't like them, you've already learned one trick. There's plenty of room outside."

OCTOBER 3, 6:12 P.M.

After dinner, the three journalists stopped by the office of the newspaper, The Antarctic Sun. Three desks, filing cabinets and a large copier pretty much filled the room.

"You'll be there," Simon said while indicating a desk with a green, plastic Hawaiian lei draped over the phone. "That's a good luck wish from last year's occupant. She seemed to think it was important to pass it on."

"Are the computers ready?" Alexia asked.

"No, they wanted to wait until we were here. I've already called and put in a request. They might be by tomorrow, the next day for sure. At least, that's what they said. Speaking of which, tomorrow's not officially a work day, so you two can do whatever you need to get settled in. I'll probably be around here most of the day, unless I get a better offer."

"Are the phones working?" JP asked.

"They should be," his boss said as he picked up a

receiver and nodded. "You know how to make a call?"

"I have it written down, along with a calling card. It's late back home, so I'll come in tomorrow morning and make a couple of calls."

"Which reminds me, here's your office key. While we're not really concerned with theft here, it's considered a good idea to keep the office locked if we're out. Besides, your room key will get lonely all by itself."

Alexia laughed at that.

"Confession time, before Simon tells the story on me anyway. I had been here at least two weeks last year before it occurred to me that there was no reason to continue carrying my car keys and home keys. I just felt naked without them."

"I understand," JP said. "The hardest thing for me right now is walking around without my cell phone."

OCTOBER 4, 7:22 A.M.

Richard and Dan were both snoring when JP crawled down from his bunk, quietly dressed and slipped away. While he and his roommates were off for a moving-in day, most of the people on station were reporting to work, so there was plenty of activity in the building.

After a breakfast even more pleasing to the reporter than dinner, he went to the newspaper office.

It was located on what some called Highway 2, which ran perpendicular to Highway 1 and was much shorter. Dominating the hall were rooms dedicated to AFRTS – Armed Forces Radio and Television Service. There was also the barber shop and a smokers' room.

He was glad to find the office empty, though he wasn't sure why he cared if someone was around while he talked on the phone. He could call from his room, but he didn't want to bother his roommates.

JP carefully reviewed his numbers and procedure. Phones were plentiful in McMurdo, including every dorm room and office. It took only a four-digit number to connect a call. Another number, though, would access a satellite uplink and give you a local phone line in Denver. So, if you were calling anyplace there, including the USAP offices, it would be, in essence, a local call.

Since his family and friends were not in Denver, he had to make a long-distance call from the stateside line. Of course, he couldn't do that directly, which meant using a calling card. So he would need to dial the outside line, key in the 800 number for the calling card, enter his card's account number, press a button or two to initiate the call, then dial his party's number. A total of 36 numbers, he counted.

"I'm a smart guy; I can do this."

Eventually, the phone was ringing.

"Hello," he heard his mother say.

"Momma, hello from Antarctica."

"Hello? Oh, there you are. JP, is that you?"

"Yes, just listen for a second. There is a delay due to the satellite uplink, so we'll have to be patient and wait for each other to respond. But it's me, Momma, I made it to Antarctica."

They talked for several minutes and he gave her one piece of information after another until she thought she had a good feel for his new life.

"There are so many people I cannot wait to tell about this," Penelope Weiscarver finally said.

"And tell them they can check the Odds and Ends newspaper online in a few days. I'll submit something every week."

JP leaned back in his chair after hanging up. That went well, he thought, and he decided to check in with Jennifer O'Hanlon. She quickly adjusted to the delay and they caught up one another on recent events, led off by her report on Bubba.

"I was hoping you'd call," she said once all the updates were in, "because I have something to get off my chest.

You've probably done so already, but I've been researching Shane Peltzer a bit. I didn't mean to, but I went back and read over your story from last spring about Professor Stapler and his research. I'll admit, I didn't really read it when it came out."

She pushed on, not giving JP time to interrupt her.

"Of course, I was intrigued by this guy, this Shane Peltzer, who up and disappeared out in the middle of literally nowhere. I mean, no body, nothing. I found that amazing. The news stories at the time were surprisingly sketchy. I ended up tracking down where he was from and read local reports there and, well, JP, it all sounds a little funny to me."

When she paused, JP waited a second trying to decide what to say.

"Let me get his straight. You did what? Goodness, Jennifer, do you have so little crime to cover on your beat that you have to go to, I don't know, where is he from?"

"Phoenix. I'm sorry if this makes you mad."

"No, no, I'm not mad, just amazed. OK, maybe I'm a little perturbed that I never checked out Peltzer, but I'm not mad. So, what sounds funny to you?"

"First of all, there's no reason for you to have checked him out; he was only a side note to your story. For me, what happened to him was more interesting than the science. But I can't exactly say what sounds funny about it. Does that seem strange? Maybe I'm finally developing my own nose for news after working with you so long."

"OK, so in addition to him being from Phoenix, what have you learned?"

"Apparently, he didn't have much in the way of friends."

"That jives with what Marcellus told me."

"But the friends he had seemed to be incredibly loyal. Combing through social media, there is a common thread that he was the best friend ever. His family, in an interview with a community paper, came out and said they believe he met with foul play. They had no evidence, mind you, just a feeling he would not have been dumb enough to walk off alone and in no way could they think of him being suicidal."

"Anything else?"

"Not really and it doesn't sound like much when I repeat it. Well, there is the point that there was so little in the news when it happened. I mean, that's the type of story that usually gets a lot of play."

"OK," JP said, measuring his words, "friends are like that because they're friends, especially if the group is a bit outside mainstream. Family is worse. I had a cop tell me back at my previous paper about a suicide years earlier in his family. He said the police investigator in him knew without a doubt that his relative killed herself, but the familial bond kept him from fully accepting it. He said that is usual for family. As for the news coverage, I agree with you more would be expected, but it did happen in the middle of the loneliest continent. If any reporter smelled a cover-up, I'd like to think there would have been much more on it."

"You're probably right. I need to hone my reporter's nose some more."

"For the other side of the coin, your reporter's nose is your best argument there's something suspicious. I'll trust instinct further than a friend's loyalty. There is one other thing, though. That's not why I'm on the Ice and, to be honest, I'm not sure my employer would welcome me digging into the story. Frankly, I'm not sure I want to play investigative reporter. I have enough to do learning to write about high-level scientific research."

"Maybe you're right to leave it be. It's not really our business."

"I'll file away your suspicions and you'll be the first to know if I come across anything that seems fishy."

As they were saying their goodbyes, JP swiveled around in his chair and saw Simon taking a seat at his desk.

"Bye-bye, Jennifer. Say hello to the crew for me and tell Stanley I'll have my first column filed in a few days. E-mail if you have any questions."

"Everyone making it without you?" Simon asked.

"I doubt it, but they'll adjust."

Simon smiled at the answer as he looked up from his startup checklist. "Shane Peltzer?"

"Yeah, I didn't know how long you'd been here. You'll remember the story I did for my home paper about the GASP project and that it mentioned Peltzer's disappearance. My co-worker found the entire scenario interesting and, apparently, her imagination has taken flight."

"What are your thoughts?" Simon asked, turning to give JP his full attention.

"That's my embarrassment, the fact I've not really given it thought. It seems I totally bought into the concept that weird things happen down here. What about you? You were around at the time."

"You will learn that being at the Antarctic newspaper does not mean you're at the center of information. Management feels no obligation to keep us updated on newsy items, particularly related to operations, unless it's good news, of course. Our best source of information, scary as it may sound, is the grapevine."

"And what did the grapevine say about Peltzer?"

"That might be the oddest part. There really was nothing. GASP is a small team and, like any such remote research party, seemed pretty closely knit. It appeared to me that they had worked through the experience as a group and, by the time they were back on station, had decided to just keep it to themselves and not relive it. I think most people respected that."

OCTOBER 4, 10:00 A.M.

Patrick Stiles was right on time to give his station

manager tour. He found five people waiting for him – four new folks and one who was returning after an eight-year absence and thought a refresher tour would be time well spent.

"Six people, that's a good number," Stiles said after introductions were made. "Let's go see what we can find.

"Oops, here's our first stop," he said after taking several steps. "On this display, you'll see the current weather situation. It's narrowed down to three labels, Condition Three, Condition Two and Condition One.

"Condition Three is normal, you feel free to come and go around the station as you wish. We've discussed leaving the station. You know when to file plans and check out radios, right? Five nodding heads, that's great. Condition Two is not good weather. You need to take care leaving a building in Condition Two.

"Condition One is absolute shutdown. If the board says One, you're not to leave the building. It doesn't happen very often during the summer season, but it can. When we get outside, I'll show you a couple of the red warning lights scattered around. If you're out and the light comes on, get yourself into the nearest building."

By then, they had worked to the side entrance at the end of Highway 2, where Stiles demonstrated how the door latches operated. Not all doors had them, but those that did needed to be properly secured to keep from blowing open and filling the place with snow during a storm.

Before exiting the building, he paused to zip up his parka and pull on leather gloves and give time for others to make their preparations. Once outside, the station manager walked a bit before stopping to talk. He had learned it takes most first-timers a little while just to come to grips with their surroundings. His first meaningful pause was in front of a large building.

"This is the Crary Science and Engineering Center, sort of the poster child for why we're here. You've heard it,

'We're here for the science.' It happens all around us, here and at field camps and the other stations. Much of those studies and accumulated information or samples find their ways here, where researchers have facilities and state-of-the-art technology to do further work. We're not going in today, but sometime you should take the opportunity to stroll through and look around."

Everyone in the group seemed ready to start moving again. JP was glad he wasn't the only one who seemed to be struggling against the cold. He had noted before leaving 155 that the outdoor temperature was minus 10 degrees Fahrenheit. When he lived up north, winter temps would drop even lower, but he had not experienced such cold for several years.

Stiles kept moving for a while, slowing down to point out the Science Support Center, Berg Field Center, the Chalet, the helicopter pads and the Chapel of the Snows. As he approached Building 165, he announced they would go inside to warm up a bit.

"Numerous operations run out of this building, but we're going to pay a visit to Mac Ops – McMurdo Operations. Think of it as communications center. How many of you are scheduled for Happy Camp the next few weeks?"

JP raised his hand and saw a couple of others did the same.

"Those of you not required to take the snow survival training can probably sign up for it later in the season after the rush subsides a bit; it's fun and full of useful information. Part of that training is operating a field radio so you can either make your scheduled check-ins or, in case of an emergency, call for help. Mac Ops is who you'll call. Right, Sunny?"

"Right you are, Patrick. That's the only reason we're stuck back in the cubbyholes of this beautiful complex. Welcome to the Ice, new guys. Don't worry about being new; it passes quickly enough. My name is Sandra DelSol, but I insist on everyone calling me Sunny. Some people think that's a reflection – get it, reflection – of my sunny personality, but that's not true. My nickname is attributable to my hometown of Naples, Florida. Patrick asked me to speak to you because I've been around for a while. Let me see, I've been here six days now. Don't laugh. Once you've been here six days, you'll swear it's been a month."

Sunny had everyone's attention as she explained Mac Ops and showed them some of the equipment. She pointed out an entry recently made for a project in the Dry Valleys, giving the time, the number of people on the site and their status.

"Then this is the most important item for us," she said while indicating a particular time. "If we've not gotten our next check-in from this camp by the designated time, it sets in motion a chain of events. First, we simply try to call them, but, to be honest, most of them are not monitoring radios in the field camps. If they are carrying a satellite phone, we'll try that. Soon, we put in a call to Patrick and that's when it gets real. Ultimately, he will dispatch a SAR team..."

"Search and rescue," Patrick interjected.

"Sorry. You see what I mean, six days ago I would never have said SAR team. When he dispatches a search and rescue team, that involves pulling all kinds of people from their regular work, commandeering vehicles and maybe helicopters that should be busy with science, and spending no small amount of money. So, what's the lesson here?"

"Don't miss a check-in," JP said, a little louder than he intended.

Sunny laughed. "It's so great when a crowd works with you."

OCTOBER 4, 11:39 A.M.

JP entered his dorm room quietly. Not knowing his

roommates yet, he was afraid someone might be asleep. Richard was gone and Dan was watching television.

"Good morning, roomie," JP said, getting a wave for a reply.

Deciding to give it one more try after hanging up Big Red and exchanging bunny boots for his normal hiking boots, JP invited Dan to join him for lunch.

"No, thanks," he replied with another wave.

JP was headed down the hallway before he mumbled, "Well, at least he'll be low maintenance."

The reporter's next thought was to pick up Simon for lunch, but the Sun office was empty. So he arrived at the galley alone.

Following him into the line, however, was Sunny DelSol.

"Hey, there, new guy, thanks for jumping in there. I was afraid I'd be left hanging. Patrick just swung by the office this morning and asked me to do that and I was scared to death it would flop."

"You were great, Sunny. You seemed like an old hand. You have an interesting job."

"It keeps us moving, though it's mostly mundane. Consider it like firefighting, you're prepared for mayhem but hoping for boredom."

"Good analogy. You're from Naples. I, too, left a view of the Gulf of Mexico to come to the Ice. Quite a change, isn't it?"

"Ah, someone who understands! Yes, I've never seen anything like this. I'm used to wearing shorts and sandals like 360 days a year. It catches my breath every time I walk outside or even look out a window."

Sunny followed JP in picking up a tray and plate as they headed toward the food. "Where are you from?"

"I was raised up north, so I have some cold weather experience, but I've been living in Oldport for more than five years now."

The food line sent them in opposite directions and JP

concentrated on filling his plate, grabbing a roll and picking out a dessert. As he turned from the tea dispenser, he saw Sunny at a small table waving him over.

"Oldport, huh?" she asked as he sat down. "My condolences on Clarice. South Florida has its share of hurricanes, but I've not seen anything like what Oldport experienced."

"Thanks. I suffered no real problems from it. Plenty of friends and acquaintances had it much worse. It made my work extremely difficult. In fact, getting the call to come down here was an enormous relief for me. Now, I'm just dealing with the guilt of leaving others behind to carry the load."

"What did you do?"

"I'm a general assignments reporter for the Odds and Ends newspaper. Still am, just on leave so I can play polar explorer."

"So you had to confront the hurricane on a personal level."

"That's a fair way to put it. You compared your job to firefighting and I guess there are similarities to reporting, as well. We do the boring things we have to do and try to stay prepared for big news. Hurricane Clarice will likely be the biggest news story I'll ever cover and, while it's exhilarating to do a tough job well, it's no fun dealing with the tragedy that is the news."

Sunny silently chewed on a tough pork chop for a few seconds.

"I understand. My father was a cop in Naples for 15 years and loved working the streets. He was good at it, I sincerely believe, and sometimes talked about staying prepared for the worst while not letting it block your view of the abounding goodness around you.

"Then, when I was 12 years old, he encountered one of those 'worst' situations, a young guy strung out on something and waving a pistol. Dad tried to talk him down, get him to drop the weapon, all the things he's supposed to do. He continued talking as the boy pointed the gun at him and pulled the trigger.

"At that point, my father's training kicked in, all the training he'd gotten in case of that worst scenario, and he shot and killed the guy. Dad did the right thing and thorough investigations confirmed it, but it haunted him for years."

"How is he now?" JP asked.

"He tried selling cars and insurance for a while, but then got hired by the Collier County Sheriff's Office as an investigator. My mom works there as a dispatcher. He's back to carrying a weapon and training for worst-case situations, but the bulk of his work is less public now than it used to be. He's happy again and he's contributing to the community again. But I relate to what you're saying."

"What about you? Has your career been in communications?"

"Heavens, no, though it's not foreign to me since my mom works in a dispatch center. No, I used to own a tanning salon. I've always been a sun worshipper and loved owning a great tan, so I started helping other people enjoy it."

"You're speaking in past-tense," JP said. "My first thought is that it's difficult to make a living selling bottled sunshine in an area where the real stuff is so readily available for free."

"Quite to the contrary, Mr. JP. I actually had a great business. My clients couldn't spend the amount of time in the sun needed to have the tans they wanted, so I kept busy and made a pretty good living. But, you're wondering why I'm on the Ice now if my business was so good. Four years ago, I was diagnosed with skin cancer ..."

"I'm sorry for jumping to conclusions, Sunny," JP blurted out.

"No problem, really. We caught it early and were able to knock it out. I was incredibly lucky, but that left me with a moral dilemma. Here I was promoting a lifestyle that proves deadly to some people, so I got out. I mean I just got out. I didn't even sell the business because I saw it as a threat to people's health. I sold the tanning beds for scrap."

"Wow, that's intense and a fantastic way to send a message. I'd like to tell your story sometime."

"Certainly," Sunny said, "but I did make the most of it. Our local paper and TV, as well as some from Tampa to Miami, did stories on it. I like to think it gave some folks pause to consider what they're doing to their skin."

"But you're fine now?"

"You know how thorough the USAP physical qualification process is. There's no way they would send me down here unless I'm cancer free and they feel I'll remain cancer free for at least a year. And I'm staying on top of it, seeing a dermatologist every six months. Anything else pops up and we'll nip it in the bud."

OCTOBER 5, 7:26 A.M.

After a day and a half of settling in, JP was more than happy to report to work. Simon was already there and Alexia walked in right behind JP.

"And the Antarctic Sun rises," Simon pronounced with considerable flourish. "First, the good news. The IT guy was in here yesterday afternoon and all three computers are updated, running and online."

"And the bad news?" Alexia asked.

"Oh, I don't know yet, but I trust it'll find us. I suggest checking your e-mail first. Mine has several things from Denver; I think Ruthann is anxious to hear from us all. Once we are caught up with the digital world, we'll see about cobbling together our action plan for the first couple of weeks."

JP was excited to see a reply from a glaciologist he wanted to interview.

"Uh, I have something from Eunice Blackburn," JP

said. "She sent this yesterday and said she's leaving at noon today for Terra Nova Bay. What's that?"

"There's an Italian base there, Mario Zucchelli Station," Simon answered. "She's using their facilities to get closer to that glacier she's studying. Not uncommon. The Italians rent rides from us to get to and from the Ice. Terra Nova is on the other side of the Ross Sea."

"I was planning on visiting with her when she returned, but should I try to see her now rather than take a chance on missing out later?"

"Bird in the hand. Got her number?"

"Yep," JP replied, already dialing. "Dr. Blackburn? This is JP Weiscarver with the, uh, The Antarctic Sun. I just opened your e-mail this morning and ... Yes, that would be great. Where do I find you? First wing to the right? Got it. Be right there."

"Wow," said Alexia, "don't you love just jumping in?"

"Ice, Oldport, wherever ... this I know how to do,"

OCTOBER 5, 7:56 A.M.

JP opened the large, heavy door on the Crary center and immediately found another set of doors. Passing through them, it was obvious he was in a different place, a special world.

The hall stretched out before him to the extent he could not see the end. He realized that was because it obviously went downhill. He remembered noticing from the outside on the previous day's tour that the building was indeed constructed on different levels running down the hillside.

There were display cases at the entryway with various Antarctic displays, but the big attention-grabber were a stuffed emperor penguin and a baby penguin inside a glass case. That is real, isn't it?

JP quickly refocused on the task at hand and proceeded a few steps until he could turn to the right down a shorter hallway. He found the scientist in a broom closet of an office, packing notebooks and other items into a bag.

"Dr. Blackburn?" he asked, standing in the doorway.

"It's Eunice, please. I'm one who likes to keep it less formal. You must be JP. Let me move these binders and you please have a seat."

The two visited a couple of minutes establishing her background and defining the purpose of glaciology before someone else appeared at the door.

"Pardon me, Dr. Eunice, but is the bag ready to go?"

"Yes, yes, I just need to add those binders. What did I do with them?"

"Were they the binders you removed from this chair?" JP asked. "You placed them on that cabinet."

"Yes, yes, there they are. Candace, meet JP. Candace is a grad student helping with this project. JP is with The Antarctic Sun and wants to tell the world what we're doing."

She completed adding the binders to the bag and gave the contents a thoughtful evaluation while the other two exchanged pleasantries. She then handed Candace the bag.

"Will this be everything?"

"That's it, Dr. Eunice. We're in good shape. Everything will be ready to go when our ride gets here."

Turning her attention back to JP once the grad student left, Eunice smiled.

"Candace spoils me. I believe she's afraid I'd not make it without her and she might be correct. Grad students are the backbone of field research. Put that somewhere in your article. We couldn't make it without them.

"Now, I was about to tell you about my research. We're headed to David Glacier, a rather large outlet glacier that flows into the Ross Sea near Terra Nova. David runs almost 100 kilometers long. Where it slowly enters the sea, it forms the Drygalski Ice Tongue."

She continued talking for 15 minutes about her project, designed to better measure the volume and speed of David

Glacier as a tool in evaluating, among other things, the changes in global weather.

"I'm thankful to have this all recorded," JP said. "I hope to be able to better understand and relate what you told me after I've been over the recording. Will you have access to your e-mail once the inevitable questions arise?"

"Yes, sure, though I might not be online every day."

"That's fine and once I'm done, I'll ask you to read over it to check for any errors."

"Of course, and maybe we can touch base again when I redeploy."

OCTOBER 5, 9:01 A.M.

"Whew," JP exclaimed as he entered the Sun office, hanging Big Red over the back of his chair and then taking a seat.

"Slow down, there, big guy," Simon said, fanning JP with a manila folder, "you've got to pace yourself. It's a long season."

"That was an amazing experience on so many levels. Are these scientists all so nice?"

"I don't know Dr. Blackburn, but to a great extent, that's true."

"Uh, she prefers 'Eunice.'"

"That's not uncommon either or, at least, most don't insist on use of titles."

"I think that's because we're all part of the same fraternity now," Alexia added. "We're all Old Antarctic Explorers, whether we're actually conducting science or making it possible for those who do. More than once I've had researchers praise those cooking food and cleaning rest rooms so the scientists can concentrate on work."

"True," Simon said, "and they appreciate what we're doing at the Sun. They're accustomed to pounding out papers for science magazines so other researchers can keep up with their work, but seldom do they get an opportunity to pass on what they've learned to the person on the street. We give them a little bit more exposure and put it in language more people understand."

"Well, I see how you can become addicted to this," JP said. "What do we do next?"

"Tomorrow, you get to go to Happy Camp!"

OCTOBER 5, 11:34 A.M.

"Hey, everyone, we got an e-mail from JP," Andrea Munoz yelled to the Odds and Ends newsroom.

Not only her message but more so the fact nobody generally heard Andrea sound off in such a fashion caused most of the heads to turn toward her.

"It's his first column for us to run. Do y'all want me to read it to you?"

"You might as well," said Stanley Hopper, "nobody's workin' now."

"OK, here goes, just imagine JP saying it"

By JP WEISCARVER
Oldport Odds and Ends
Outside my window is ice and snow ... for hundreds of miles and some of it thousands of years old.

Yes, after a whirlwind of events, I recently arrived in Antarctica, thinking, "My gosh, what have I done?"

I entered this little adventure knowing fully well that it may be one of the most exciting and invigorating things I've done or ... possibly ... a time of misery and regret. I decided it was a risk worth taking. After all, I said numerous times to myself and others, it's less than five months and a person can do anything for a determined amount of time.

Whether taking a writing job on the Ice at the bottom of the world was a good or bad decision will form slowly; there is no rush to reach a conclusion, partly because it will have no effect on the situation. However, one suspicion has already proven true. The people are incredible.

There is no norm among the people who are providing support services for the scientific research going on here. Many are young, in their 20s. That's understandable, as most have no children. There is a good chance they are not married and, if they are, that their spouses are also involved. On the other hand, not a small number of the participants are older, even older than me. Many are single, but quite a few have left at home spouses, boyfriends or girlfriends, children and other family.

And one learns to not read too much into job descriptions.

One new friend is a spring college graduate with a degree in mechanical engineering. She accepted a job here that will entail replacing light bulbs, shoveling snow, etc. I don't know the pay, but it's a lot less than any engineering job. Why did she take the position?

"It's just cool," she said. "I mean, how often do you get an opportunity to do something like this?"

Like me, she is a first-timer. Many here are, but an awful lot of people come back year after year, sometimes taking a year off and then returning. Deep friendships are obvious.

Whether walking the hallways of the dorm or crossing between buildings while bundled against subzero temperatures and modest winds, people greet each other. Introductions to veterans, almost without fail, end with a wish like, "Hope you have a great season."

The presence of incredible people is no surprise, of course. You and I both know plenty of amazing folks wherever we live ... good people who are kind, courteous and helpful. If they are found everywhere, then they must be found in Antarctica, but the harsh environment seems to bring them even closer together.

That is something I do not expect to change much through the season.

- - 30 - -

"What's the '30' mean?" Andrea asked.

"It's old school, my dear," replied Pat Baird. "It indicates the end of the article. He's probably just showing off to Stanley and me."

"He does sound happy," Jennifer O'Hanlon said.

"Yeah, yeah and we're all happy for him," Stanley said while waving folks away from Andrea's desk. "What I see is a guy who can mess up my deadlines even when he's thousands of miles away. Back to work, boys and girls."

3 HAPPY CAMP

OCTOBER 6, 7:55 A.M.

As instructed, JP arrived at the SSC – the Science Support Center – decked out in his extreme weather gear. If he wasn't wearing it, he had it in his orange bag.

He found the classroom, hung his parka with the others outside and placed his bag underneath. Inside the small lecture room, several people were already gathered, partaking of sweet rolls and coffee. JP joined them even though he ate a nice breakfast two hours earlier.

Soon enough, it became obvious who was in charge as a man and a woman, both about JP's age, gave directions on arranging chairs and ordering gear to be left outside.

"Good morning," said the woman, repeating the greeting as things quieted down. The second time, she received a hearty reply.

"Oh, wow, that's great," she said.

"My name is Natalie Skinner. I am an instructor with the Field Safety Training Program and will be your lead instructor for this ... come now, you know what we call it ... Happy Camp! This is Brian Embers. He's also an instructor and every bit as qualified as me, but we just take

60

turns playing lead. Either one of us should be able to help you with a question or an issue."

"What is Happy Camp?" Brian asked. "Is it just a party? Or is it such an arduous and trying experience that people gave it a deceptively pleasant name just to get people to show up?"

He looked around the room briefly and settled on Natalie.

"The answer to those questions would be 'yes,'" she said. "It's fun but not easy."

"It's serious training," Brian picked up, giving the feel the two of them had been through this routine several times. "Happy Camp is snow survival school. If your job requires you to leave the McMurdo area, you are required first of all to have survival training. The good news is you're cleared for five years with nothing more than a short annual refresher course."

"What about going to Scott Base?" came a question from one of the 20 campers.

"That rude interruption reminds me that you're encouraged to rudely interrupt us anytime you have a question. Scott Base, which you probably know, is the New Zealand base just a couple of miles away. As long as we're under Category 3 weather, you're free to walk or ski to Scott."

"Or take the Thursday shuttle," Natalie said.

"Yes, Thursday is American night at Scott. You'll see their kiwi green buildings as we drive out to our campsite this morning. Let's see, the objective of Happy Camp is to equip you with the knowledge to have a chance to survive should you be temporarily stranded on the coldest, windiest, highest and driest continent on earth."

"Does this cover eating each other in order to survive?"

"No, that's in the advanced course."

OCTOBER 6, 10:22 A.M.

The classroom segment of Happy Camp was maddening. Everyone came dressed for cold weather but spent two hours inside a heated room, where the advice included the warning to not let yourself get so warm that you sweat. That body moisture would come back to haunt you when it started to freeze against your body.

The information was good, including commands to keep up food and water intake. The body must have fuel to generate heat. Water is often overlooked because of the cold, but it's necessary to keep everything functioning well.

Tips abounded, from how to layer clothing to storing one's water bottle inside the parka to keep it from freezing.

When word arrived that transportation was outside, the campers dressed out and hauled their bags to the two vehicles out back – a passenger Delta and the terra bus. The wind had picked up considerably and the blowing snow stung JP's face. From the storeroom, campers acquired and loaded two team bags, a few tents and sleeping bags for everyone.

The ride off the station was slow and crowded. The promised glimpse of the Kiwi base was not very fulfilling due to the cramped conditions, frosted windows and blowing snow. The drivers veered left before entering Scott. First stop would be out on the Ross Ice Shelf.

OCTOBER 6, 12:15 P.M.

Once the vehicles arrived, campers were ordered to quickly unload everything for the drivers had to pick up incoming passengers on the sea ice. JP was one of those who climbed to the top of the Delta to toss bags onto the snow.

Taking a moment to look around from his vantage point, he was confident they were indeed in the middle of nowhere. The only manmade objects he could see were several tall flags sticking out of the snow. Of course, he realized, he probably couldn't see more than 25 yards.

As transportation drove off, Natalie and Brian yelled above the noisy wind for the campers to grab the boxes of sack lunches, as well as their personal bags and to follow them to the instruction hut, called, even more simply, the I-hut.

Chatter soon gave way to mostly silence as the 22 "survivors" followed a line of flags for at least a quarter of a mile. Eventually, a small portable building came into view. Brian held the door as the campers walked in, kicking and shaking off snow as best they could.

First order of business was passing out sack lunches and allowing everyone to eat. Next came even more lecture, including how to operate the camp stoves, which would be needed for future meals.

Through the session, everyone took a turn to visit the outhouse. It was just that, a simple shelter with a seat positioned over a large, deep hole in the otherwise pristine glacial ice.

About the time everyone felt warm, they were commanded to trudge back to the campsite. It was time to put the happy into Happy Camp.

OCTOBER 6, 3:09 P.M.

JP was amazed how much the weather had deteriorated since their arrival. Or had it?

"I have a question," he said to instructor Brian as they worked their way through the snow. "Is this normal weather? I mean, this seems pretty bad to me, but, then again, it seldom even freezes where I come from."

"This is normal for this time of year," Brian said, obviously breathing easier than JP, "but it's not common. That is, you're going to see days like this, but they don't come up too often. We're in, I'd guess, a Condition 2 right now. This is a great opportunity. If we survive this, we'll be better prepared to take on a real emergency."

"If?" JP yelled above the wind.

Brian laughed and continued looking for the next flag.

Things got busy once they arrived at the drop point. Their bags were all deposited in one spot to minimize the possibility of losing one in the blowing snow, and campers began putting up the first of two Scott Polar tents, the iconic Antarctic shelter that pre-dated U.S. exploration of the continent.

The process went slowly as Natalie and Brian provided instruction and oversight along the way.

Campers learned how to make a dead-man anchor to secure lines in the snow. They shoveled snow onto the wide valances of the tent shell to secure a seal. Everyone pitched in at times and watched at others, all the while trying to keep warm and keep their goggles clear enough to see. Once the first was up, the second tent followed in short order.

Each Scott tent would sleep three that night. Seven two-man mountaineering tents went up more quickly and, like that, the campers had somewhere to sleep that night.

Next order of business was to build a wall out of snow bricks.

They picked an area a bit out of the way and brushed off some of the loose snow to get down to packed snow. For the first time, JP grasped an understanding of glacial development.

A glacier is a huge sheet of ice, but its growth comes slowly as years of snowfalls are packed by later snowfalls until they are solid ice. As the ice gets deeper, it gets heavier, eventually reaching the point that gravity forces its creeping crawl toward lower levels. In the case of the Ross Ice Shelf, on which JP was standing, it is formed by glacial ice reaching the Ross Sea. It floats there, ever so slowly working its way to warmer waters, eventually melting away or breaking free.

Thinking about the ancient, deep ice underneath his feet did nothing to make JP feel more comfortable. Standing there – trying to keep his back to the wind, sheltering his face, struggling to breathe through his neck gaiter, fighting frost buildup on his goggles – he found he was daydreaming about escaping the cold.

JP refocused when it came his turn to wield the saw – a standard, old carpenter's saw – to slice through the packed snow. The most amazing thing was the sound. It seemed the ice cried as the saw cut a path. The eerie sound, which he likened to recordings of a whale's song, penetrated the howling of the wind.

Each ice block was lifted and placed on a sled that was periodically pulled to the wall. The idea was to construct a barrier to keep some of the wind and snow from buffeting the tents during the night.

After JP took a turn sawing and helped pull a load of blocks to the wall, he turned toward one of the Scott tents and worked his way inside, taking a minute to figure out the collapsed chute of an entryway, a design to keep snow from blowing in.

Inside, he found the escape he sought. The extreme weather was beginning to get to him, he realized. It was a degree of frozen misery he had never imagined. Indeed, he found himself wondering if he could cut it.

He was roused from his self-pity by Brian crawling into the tent.

"How's it going, JP?" the instructor asked, glancing at JP's nametag on Big Red. "You doing all right?"

"I'm not so sure, Brian. I thought I was fairly tough. I rode out a hurricane less than two months ago, but this, this is beating me down."

"It's OK, buddy. We're throwing a lot at you. Hurricane Clarice? Man, that was one bad storm. So, do you live on the Gulf coast?"

The two of them chatted for a couple of minutes while Brian took JP's goggles from his hand, extracted a bandanna and cleaned them. The reporter recognized what his instructor was doing – talking him down from his anxiety, discerning his problems, offering advice – and he appreciated the help and Brian's skill.

His final move was to help JP get his clothing situated to help protect his face without fogging his goggles too badly.

"You ready to get back at it?" he asked.

"Go ahead; I'll be a couple of seconds behind you."

As Brian worked his way out of the chute, JP rose to his knees, shook himself and said out loud, "Get it done, Weiscarver."

Outside, he slapped Brian on the back, gave him a thumb's-up and started stacking bricks onto the wall.

OCTOBER 6, 11:18 P.M.

All the work and worry had faded into the past as Bob (JP wasn't even trying to learn last names) capped off the evening with a tale of camping in grizzly bear country. He managed to turn a scary encounter into a funny story. JP sat quietly in one corner, glad to soak up the warmth and good times of the others.

The instructors were a distant memory, having left the campers before dinnertime, following the flags back to the I-hut, where they would enjoy a heater for the evening. The wind never did let up and their red parkas promptly disappeared.

Once they were gone, the campers took charge and set up two camp stoves, one in each Scott tent. Fresh snow was gathered in large metal pans and melted over the fire. Tending the pot had been JP's job. They continued adding snow until there was plenty of hot water to pour into each person's meal packet.

"This isn't half bad," Katie said.

"Of course," added JoAnn, "this tent would probably taste pretty good right now."

They took turns encouraging each other to eat plenty. They knew their bodies would need the fuel to keep warm during the night.

Enough snow was melted to provide warm water to refill bottles. Finally, the stoves were broken down and stored.

JP ended up assigned to sleep in the Scott tent where he had been heating water. He would share it with Glenn and Katie, but it also attracted a lot of company. They were laughing, telling stories, speculating on tomorrow's weather and simply enjoying the fact they had successfully made camp in such a challenging environment.

Someone, as Bob finished his grizzly story, spoke over the din, "How did we get 20 people in here?" JP hadn't really noticed. He was tired but comfortable.

After a while, they began leaving for their own tents. Of course, it was still daylight since the sun barely dipped below the horizon this time of year, but the blowing snow gave everything a muted appearance.

JP made one more visit to the outhouse, which was identical to the one at the I-hut, and he and his roommates spread out three sleeping bags, pretty much filling the tent floor.

The night was uneventful. JP awoke often and, all night, a glow from the sun lit up the orange tent. When he was cold, he "ran" in his sleeping bag, pumping his legs and arms while lying on his back. He would extract his water bottle from inside the warm sleeping bag and take a few sips. He also snacked on peanut M&Ms, a package of which he had tucked into the bib pocket of his coveralls. The treat lasted all night and he envisioned it as giving his body fuel to keep warm.

Glenn, who was an experienced highland camper, seemed to sleep straight through the night; JP never noticed him moving. Katie, who was on the other side of JP, tossed and turned a bit and one time made a run to the outhouse.

More than once, JP slipped back into sleep thinking, "I cannot believe I'm sleeping on an ice shelf."

OCTOBER 7, 7:11 A.M.

Once morning came, the campers emerged to find clear skies and much more comfortable conditions. JP set to work boiling water for breakfast and they soon began striking camp. Before they were through, the instructors walked up and complained they were running late.

"Yeah, we missed you, too," Bob yelled out.

The night was done but instruction remained.

There was a lesson on using field radios and they made a call to Mac Ops. There was the bucket drill, where several campers had plastic buckets placed over their heads to resemble whiteout conditions where they could not see or clearly hear each other but had to practice completing a task.

They were in the middle of setting up a practice camp when an instructor's radio came to life.

"Stow everything away and get your gear gathered," Natalie yelled. "Transport will be here in 10 minutes. They have a scheduling issue and need to get us out of here ASAP."

A cheer arose from 20 weary campers as they began following their final orders.

OCTOBER 7, 1:11 P.M.

JP received his own cheer when he carried his bag into the Sun office.

"We were a little worried about you yesterday," Alexia said. "That was a decent little storm and not one I'd want to be riding out in a tent."

"It was no problem once we got into our tents," JP said, trying to not swell too much but enjoying the glory. "The tough part was setting up camp in the storm. I don't mind saying I wasn't sure I wanted to be there."

Simon told him to take a hot shower and rest up.

"Don't worry. It's standard practice to take off the rest

of the day. We need you ready to go tomorrow."

After grabbing a late lunch, JP did just that.

Program participants were encouraged to limit showers in both number and duration in order to minimize water usage. The threat of rationing was publicized, though JP understood it to be rare. He played his part, however, spreading out showers and keeping them quick.

His post-Happy Camp shower, though, took a little bit longer; the warm water felt too good.

OCTOBER 12, 8:44 A.M.

JP's mind wandered as he was reading background information about yet another scientist he was planning to interview.

He had only been working here a week or so, but it seemed like months. He remembered what Sunny DelSol said during the introductory tour, "Once you've been here six days, you'll swear it's been a month."

Smiling, he was stretched out in his chair when Simon walked in.

"My, but you sure do look contented. Ready for a little break?"

"Sure, what's up?"

"Didn't you volunteer for the MCI team?"

"MCI? Oh, uh, mass casualty incident, right? I signed up for the walking blood bank and to work as a stretcher bearer. Is something wrong?"

"No, but I just heard through the grapevine that we're about to have an MCI drill."

At that time, all three phones started ringing. The repeated message was, "All MCI team members are to report to the fire station."

Simon and JP were getting their parkas when Alexia walked in.

"MCI drill," Simon said. "Did you volunteer this year?"

"Are you kidding? They wouldn't dare have a disaster

without me," she said, turning on her heels.

"I have a camera for photos," JP said, following her out the door.

OCTOBER 13, 5:35 P.M.

"No, it was far from exciting," JP told Jennifer the next day. "The scenario was an explosion on the ice runway. Some of the stretcher bearers went out to help load victims. I stayed back partly because I didn't take my bunny boots."

"I laugh every time I hear 'bunny boots,'" she said.

"Anyway, I stood around the fire station forever, helped move some things to set up treatment areas, etc. When the victims arrived, we moved them. Like I said, not all that exciting."

"After Happy Camp, I suppose a lot of things aren't exciting," she said. "I saw your column today and you made it sound almost too miserable to deal with, but I'm glad you did."

"As am I, Jen. Had I been dropped off in such a situation, even with all of the survival gear but without the Happy Camp training, I would have been a dead duck. My brain would have frozen with fear and my body would have soon followed. But we are a hardier species than that."

"Any additional insight into whether Shane Peltzer could have survived?"

"I've thought about that. It doesn't seem likely he would have been prepared. According to what little I've heard, the prevailing theories were that he wandered off and didn't return either because of an accident or because he had no intention of coming back."

"Even if he did commit suicide, I wish they would have found his body, just to help his family deal with it."

"They did look, but it truly is a harsh environment."

OCTOBER 14, 6:57 A.M.

"Hey, honey, I think you'd enjoy reading this."

"Yeah, did some politician admit he didn't have a clue and resign?"

"Moose" MacDuff had a two-day break, the first since Hurricane Clarice. As a supervising lineman for the Oldport Regional Electric Cooperative, his life had revolved around getting Oldport County completely up and running again. Reading the newspaper wasn't exactly on his agenda today.

"OK, maybe it's not that good," said his wife, Kathy, "but a man's man like you can probably relate."

She tossed him the paper, folded to JP's column.

By JP WEISCARVER
Oldport Odds and Ends
Less than 72 hours into my Antarctic experience found me bundled in my ECW – extreme cold weather gear – along with 19 others as we prepared camp in the snow atop a glacial ice shelf.

They call it Happy Camp and the sarcasm is deeper than the ice.

We lucked out with our camping experience because the weather gradually deteriorated all day as we pitched tents and built a wall made of "bricks" sawed out of the packed snow. Temperatures were down to about 20 degrees below zero, but the winds that drove horizontal snow brought the wind chill much lower.

Lucky? Why?

Because, if we survived – and survival is actually pretty well guaranteed, regardless how miserable we felt – the story of camping out in Antarctica would be all that much better. That fact was borne out after we returned to station. Over the next few days, if the topic of Happy Camp came up – and I was not hesitant to bring it up – people said all the right things. They knew we had a challenging experience.

Yep, that was us. We met the storm and we survived.

But, I confided in friends, I felt more like a survivor by default. Had there been a bus stop nearby, it's quite possible I would have boarded transport to shelter from the cold and wind that made every task from breathing to seeing a trying and wretched experience.

But there's more to walking out than easing one's own discomfort. It's ... well ... it's quitting.

I remember vividly my high school football coach. He had a saying: "A quitter is a quitter is a quitter." Simple but effective.

Yeah, I thought of Coach during Happy Camp. If I resigned and moved into the instructors' hut, one less person would be available the next morning to break camp. My job wasn't huge, but I had a part. We were a team and everyone played a role.

"It's only for a short while," I said to myself. "Just get through the next task. You don't want to tell people you freaked out and quit on Happy Camp."

Indeed, another thought playing across my mind was that the entire experience would make a great story to tell. Isn't that pretty much what brought me to Antarctica in the first place? A desire to encounter new things, to take advantage of a rare opportunity to see and do things most people don't.

So, I toughed it out, managed to get through. I leaned on teammates when necessary and, I think, did a fair job of carrying my share of the load.

With all due apologies to Robert Frost, I took the road less traveled by with hopes it will make all the difference.

"Hmph," Moose said as he tossed the paper onto the table. "Sounds like fun."

OCTOBER 20, 5:57 P.M.

Well into his third week on the Ice, JP had definitely

fallen into the schedule, particularly the meals.

Eating in the galley was fun, simple as that. The food was dependably good and there was always a nice selection, including dessert.

Sure, maybe he would tire of it eventually, but the bachelor in him was determined to enjoy it for all it was worth.

He was running a little later than usual for dinner since he hung around the office a bit after the usual 5:30 quitting time in order to polish a story. He found he reworked stories more here, primarily to make sure the science presented in them was solid.

Approaching 6 p.m., he dashed up the stairs to his dorm room, unlocked the door and found his third roommate had arrived.

"Hello there, we've been wondering when you'd get here," JP blurted out to the young man watching television from the sofa.

The newcomer jumped up from his perch, stuck out his right hand and said, "Howdy, sir, my name's Dwight Mooney."

"Whoa, there, buddy," JP said, grasping the extended hand. "Let me give you a hint. You'd best drop that 'sir' business around here, especially if you're talking to me. There's not much of a social hierarchy on the Ice."

"Yes, sir, I'm forever working on that. What's your name."

"See what I mean, your double-sir blew me out of the water and I forgot to introduce myself. JP Weiscarver."

"What does the JP stand for?" Dwight asked.

"Nothing, never has, never will. What are you doing here?"

"I'm a mechanic, I'll be working nights performing preventive maintenance on the various fleet. You?"

"Uh, I'm a journalist writing about research and life on the Ice and, uh, I'm working days, like both of our other roommates. I cannot believe they do this."

"Bunk day workers and night workers together? I know; it drove us crazy last year, too. I gave up trying to get them to change it."

"So, you're an old-timer. This your second season?"

"Yep. I'm a good roommate, I'll tell you, but just like you guys, I work hard and need my sleep."

"We're not the first to do this; we'll make it work. I'm headed to dinner. Care to join me?"

En route to the galley, they met Dan on his way back to the room.

"How old are you, son?" Dan asked, ever his charming self.

"I'm 22, pops. How old are you?"

Dan actually laughed at the response.

"I'm 56 and I totally deserve that comeback."

"Yeah, Dan, you do need to show a little respect here," JP contributed. "You're talking to a wily Ice veteran."

While JP and Dwight worked through the food line, Richard came by replenishing the supply of green peas and brief introductions were made.

"It just occurred to me," JP said to Dwight as they sat down, "that we already had a small sleeping schedule conflict in our room. Richard often has to go to work at 4 a.m. and sometimes works the overnight meal, what do they call it?"

"Midrats, another holdover of Navy lingo, short for midnight rations. Working nights would be tough without it."

"So, yeah, we'll make it work just fine."

OCTOBER 28, 5:43 A.M.

"Jay, we got another e-mail from JP," Penelope Weiscarver yelled toward the next room.

"We hear from him more now that he's in Antarctica than when he was on the coast," he said while pulling up a chair.

"Well, it's not that he wrote us but he copied his column to us again."

"I know, but we can pretend, can't we? I'll just read over your shoulder."

By JP WEISCARVER
Oldport Odds and Ends

With the exception of leaving my family and friends for a few months, my single greatest concern about working in Antarctica was not the cold, the long hours, the isolation from the "real world." My biggest worry was having a roommate. Hands down, that was the most intimidating thought.

I haven't shared a home with anyone in years. Even in college, with the exception of one summer semester, I always had my own bedroom. So the idea of living and sleeping in the same room with some stranger, not to mention sharing a bathroom down the hall with dozens of guys, gave me pause.

Wait, did I say someone else? No, no, no. It ended up being three other guys and me in one room. Two bunk beds, closets, some furniture and just enough room to walk between them. Then, to top things off, one of the guys works overnight and sleeps during the day.

A month into the experience, I am pleasantly surprised to be able to say that it's working out rather well.

Success lies in the fact that we are all easy-going and considerate of each other. If anyone is in bed, the others take it easy with the lights and keep the television on low volume. None of us is much of a party animal. We consult each other on what to have on television, which is easy since the choice is between two movies, sports, news or a network TV catchall channel.

Our ages differ considerably, something like 22-29-40-56, but we don't treat Dan like an old man or Dwight like a kid. We will sometimes go out to do something together and will often share a table at meals. And we talk about things – mostly families, friends and lives left behind.

Yeah, I like them all.

However, when you live this closely with people, you start to notice things.

Dan, for example, is a bit of a hermit. That might not be totally fair because, as a plumber, he often spends a decent amount of his work day outside. Working outside in Antarctica can certainly leave someone wanting to kick back and relax afterwards, so that may explain why he's almost always lying in his bed watching DVDs he brought from home or playing computer games.

I guess my only problem with Dan is that I cannot really get to know him.

I'll find him lying in his bed, wearing earphones and watching an old movie and, after a while, I'll try to ask him a question. I've inquired about what he was watching, where he's from, what's happening at work, etc., and get the simplest, bluntest answers, usually some form of yes, no or his favorite, I don't know.

Richard, on the other hand, is a talking machine when he's not working. On the rare occasion I find something I'd like to watch on TV, I have to consider if Richard will be home or not.

Suffice it to say there is no quiet time when Richard is in the room.

I'm not complaining, mind you, just observing. I really enjoy talking with him, especially if I can get him going about one of the many odd temporary jobs he's had over the years. If not, well, stand by for a blow-by-blow description of the number of onions he chopped at work today. If it makes him feel better about having to slice and dice tear-makers, I'm glad to lend an ear.

Dwight is our new roommate. He's the 22-year-old and yet the only one of our group who's worked on the Ice before.

Bottom line, from my perspective, it's nice that if we have a day-sleeper it's someone who's worked out the details in the past and doesn't mind laying out a plan. What I don't like is that I would enjoy visiting with Dwight more. Maybe on Sundays.

So, while it hasn't been easy, it's working. We're all getting along. By the end of the season, we may all four be great friends.

- - 30 - -

"Sounds like Richard might be good training for being married," JP's father said.

"Hush, Jay."

NOVEMBER 8, 9:13 A.M.

"Hey, JP," Simon called out without even looking over his shoulder. "I see on the passenger manifest that the GASP team is arriving today. Have you made contact with them, scheduled an interview?"

"Contact, yes; interview, no. We traded e-mails the other day before they left Denver and I'll touch base with him while they're here, but the interview won't be until they're redeploying."

"Oh, yeah, I remember. You had already talked to him after last season and you're waiting in order to have new and better information. I see it now. We have that story penciled in for the last week in January."

"But I do have an appointment with Eunice Blackburn this morning. She's on her way home in two days, so we're going to review her observations in order to tie up the David Glacier article. I already have it pretty much written. I told her it would be to her by first thing tomorrow and she promised to have it back before dinner. In other words, it should be ready for the next publication cycle."

"Cool. Meanwhile, Alexia, I'd like each of you to read over my lead to the artist feature. Something's not clicking and I'm having trouble seeing it. I'd like your feedback."

4 THE PENGUIN FLIES

NOVEMBER 9, 7:04 A.M.

More than a month into his season, JP was still in love with breakfast on the Ice. Lunch and dinner were good, but breakfast always started him off on the right foot.

There was always scrambled eggs – probably fake eggs but still tasty – and often a specialty egg, such as one with jalapenos or potatoes or something. There would usually be pancakes, maybe with M&Ms or blueberries, or French toast or waffles. Some breakfast meat was available every morning, maybe bacon, sausage or ham.

JP headed toward the coffee urn with a tray carrying three fluffy pancakes with syrup, two sausage patties, a generous scoop of scrambled eggs, a mixture of cantaloupe and muskmelon chunks and a small glass of orange juice.

Over his line of sight toward the coffee mugs, he saw an extended arm waving back and forth. The arm was attached to Marcellus Stapler.

"My good man, you look as if you've settled into Ice life marvelously," Stapler said as JP approached the large table. "Please join us. I'd like to introduce the team to JP Weiscarver, my reporter friend from Oldport I've been telling you about."

"If I'm not interrupting high-level planning from the GASP think tank," JP said as he took a seat.

"No, man, we're just enjoying a meal where Marcellus can't stick us for the tab," popped off one of the team members.

"Thank you, Josh, for identifying yourself as the class clown, so we'll start with Joshua Smith, our support lead who also drove our primary tractor last year."

"Oh, I forgot to tell you I'll be driving the airplane this year," Josh said, a remark that earned him a slug in the shoulder.

"Our enforcer there is one of our grad students, Jackson Merkel," Stapler continued. "Next is MaryLu Hatcher, our principal investigator, the boss with whom you will wish to confer upon our return. This is Chris Begin, the fellow researcher who makes up for my poor contributions. Over here is support assistant Terry Masters, who is the team's only new member this year. Here is our other grad student, Rick Tomkins, and finally, near my side and even closer to my heart, the person who kept us alive with her wonderful field camp culinary skills, cook Karen Watkins."

Stapler finished the elaborate introductions with a celebratory gesture, as if he was about to take a bow, when he realized everyone was inordinately subdued.

"What? Did I miss ... oh, 'keeping us alive.' Sorry, my friends, a most unfortunate slip on my part. You know what I meant."

"We do, Marcellus," said MaryLu Hatcher. "We all understand. It's just awkward being back here."

"Indeed," contributed Chris Begin. "I thought I had put that all behind me, but, uh, I'm sorry, does our guest even know what we're talking about?"

JP nodded while swallowing. "Your lost team member from last year?"

"Yes. Anyway, I found a lot of strange feelings once I

stepped off the plane and looked out on that expanse of ice."

"Seeing the ice and snow again made real what had come to feel like a bad dream," said Rick Tomkins.

"Wow," said Jackson Merkel, "I'm thinking maybe we should call in the school counselors."

"That's enough, Jackson," MaryLu stated with authority. "It was a piece of trauma we all had to deal with in our own ways. I'm sure we all would rather leave it in our past and move on, but how to do so will differ. And, yes, Jackson does have a point. If anyone wants to talk about it, at any time, I wish you'd come see me."

After a moment of silence, Karen and Terry excused themselves and Rick soon followed after them, leaving the table quiet except for JP's fork against his plate.

"So, did you have any trouble finding the place?" JP asked, getting a laugh from Chris, a smile from Hatcher and a nod of appreciation from Stapler.

"Everything came together beautifully," Josh said, glancing around the table. "It was as if Hoyle wrote the guidebook."

"Hey, that was my line," Stapler objected while Jackson and Josh exchanged a high-five.

"It does sound like something Marcellus would say," JP acknowledged.

"Indeed he did," Jackson said, "but Hoyle clearly stated in the guidebook that clever lines left on the table are free for appropriation by quickly thinking opponents." That meant another high-five.

"Argh, hoisted by my own petard," Stapler dramatically exclaimed, bringing the celebration to a pause while Jackson and Josh exchanged quizzical looks.

MaryLu laughed out loud.

"Indeed, it looks as if the good professor here has upped the ante," she said, "and you gentlemen have a little homework to do if you're staying in the game."

Jackson and Josh mumbled as they carted off their

trays. "What's a petard?" "I'm off to check the rules according to Google."

"When do y'all get started?" JP asked the three lead researchers.

"We've given everyone, including ourselves, this morning to relax and get acclimated just a bit," Chris said. "After lunch, we have some training at Berg Field Center. Fortunately, while Terry is new to our team, he's worked here before and none of us has to go through Happy Camp. That saves us two days."

"All of us have to take the refresher course," MaryLu said, "which is tomorrow, by the way."

"But you probably are inquiring about our departure time; we're scheduled to fly out on the 15th," Marcellus said, looking at his watch. "Today is the ninth, so we're already running behind."

"Relax, we're fine," MaryLu said as if she had been saying it all along. "There's not near as much to do this year in the way of preparations. Except for Terry, we've all done it before."

"Don't worry about Terry," Chris added. "He's already made himself a nice fit in the team and will certainly be an improvement."

The other two turned to look at him at that comment.

"Hey, I'm sorry. No disrespect, but we all know it's true." That brought a slight nod from both of them and JP rose from his chair.

"I've had my acclimation time, I'm afraid, and they're expecting me in the office. In fact, I'm running a little late."

"No worries, my lad," Marcellus said. "You were already at work. Asked us some probing questions, you did."

"I'll go with that. Thanks."

NOVEMBER 11, 11:49 A.M.

The Rev. Ann Dickenson turned away from a program outline she was struggling to pull together and looked out her window onto the streets of Oldport. The community seemed strong but tired almost three months since Hurricane Clarice's devastation.

Ann knew she was tired, but she also knew many dealt with difficulties greater than hers.

Not yet ready to return to work, she picked up the Odds and Ends newspaper and absentmindedly thumbed through it until JP's dispatch from Antarctica caught her eye.

By JP WEISCARVER
Oldport Odds and Ends
Being one of only a few thousand people on the entire continent of Antarctica would, on its surface, suggest things are quite roomy. Looking at the big picture, yes, that's one person for every 1,000 square miles or so. You could go many hundreds of miles in some cases without finding anyone else.

That is, once you get off station – out of town, so to speak. However, life on station is anything but lonely.

Everyone at McMurdo Station, with a very few possible exceptions, has one or more roommates. Some of the upper-class dorms have restrooms shared by two dorm rooms. Others, like mine, have men's and women's restrooms on each floor, shared by everyone. For example, it's not uncommon to have to wait for a shower to open up.

That's not as bad as it sounds because, frankly, people don't shower as much here. To be honest, as one fellow told me, the low temperatures and low humidity greatly decrease the "stink factor."

Meals are in a large dining room. It's nicer than what you remember from school, but it's definitely not cozy. A person can fill a plate, cover it with plastic wrap and take it back to the room to eat, but that's a bit of trouble and, besides, don't forget the roommates.

There is no restaurant, by any common definition of the term. The only alternative to the galley is the fact that, two or three nights a week, burgers are served up at one of the bars. Buying a hamburger, though it is not expensive, does mean that you're shelling out money instead of eating the meal that is free. However, it is worth the few bucks every few weeks just for the change of pace. Even so, you're still eating with a bunch of other people and in a noisier environment.

The cold weather – particularly if it's windy – discourages one from seeking solitude outside for very long.

Those who knew me best expressed some concern for me living in an almost communal environment. While I immensely like being around people, I do thoroughly enjoy time to myself. Or time visiting with my ferret buddy, Bubba.

I must admit that it hasn't been all that bad here. The biggest reason may be the people are so interesting.

There is a janitor who spent more than three months in a third-world country after a killer tsunami almost two years ago. He directed the building of houses for those who lost their homes. Another janitor lived in Senegal for quite some time and has been active in fighting against the horrendous practice commonly known as female circumcision.

One of my best friends has been a fellow who tried to come down for the previous summer season but learned during the physical that he had cancer. Surgery and chemotherapy kept him from coming, yet he worked hard through rehab and qualified to come this year.

A woman has served as a mountain climbing guide all over the world. A young man has hitchhiked in 43 countries, covering more than 60,000 miles.

I am probably among the least-traveled people here. I've been over much of the United States, but many of my co-workers have done that and visited a large number of other countries. And most of them are not just tourists – toting cameras and hitting the hot spots. They are more likely to get down to what makes a different culture tick, seeing things at street-level and getting to know common folks.

With stories like that to hear, it seems a shame to spend too much time seeking solitude.

"Good for you, my friend," Pastor Ann said as she folded the paper. "Your eyes have been opened, all the better for you to see the truths of this wondrous world we inhabit."

NOVEMBER 14, 6:01 P.M.

JP hurried through dinner, returned to his room to put on his wind pants and, after consideration, even his bunny boots. He had high hopes for the evening and didn't want his lack of preparation to cut it short. Of course, he grabbed Big Red, which always had a pair of gloves, his neck gaiter, a warm knit cap and some other handy pieces.

"Oh, I can't forget my camera."

As he headed to the door, Richard came in.

"Hey, JP, I just heard there are some penguins down by Hut Point. I'm going to grab some grub and head down there. Want to come with? I hope they're Emperors."

"Way ahead of you, Richard. I've had dinner and am headed out. I'd offer to wait for you, but I'm afraid I might miss them. It's awfully early in the season for them to show up, I understand."

"No problemo, dude. I'm tempted to go with you, but I only had a sack lunch and don't want to miss dinner."

"See you later. Oh, I'm told they're Adelies, not Emperors."

"I don't really care ... they're penguins!"

JP took the back door of Building 155 and scooted between some dorms and the galley's storage buildings to take the road around Winter Quarters Bay to Hut Point.

Hut Point's name comes from a small building located past the ice pier. Discovery Hut was built in 1902 as part of Robert Falcon Scott's Discovery Expedition and was utilized by different expeditions off and on for 15 years. After the U.S. Navy established McMurdo Station in 1956, the hut was dug out of snow and ice and preserved for its historical significance.

JP could see the crowd of people around the point as soon as it came into sight, but it was a while before he could definitely make out the small black and white penguins. As he passed the ice pier, he slowed his pace so he could better watch the continent's trademark animal, often stopping to snap a photo, even before he was really close enough to do any good.

As he neared Discovery Hut, he saw a few dozen penguins hanging out on the edge of the ice, occasionally coming and going through a hole into the sea. That's also where most of the watchers were and JP couldn't help but notice they were all behaving themselves quite well.

It was drilled into program participants that they were not to interact with or bother any wildlife. The clearest example was often restated as, "If you're close enough the animal reacts to you, then you're too close."

Of course, everybody wanted to get close to a penguin and it's often said penguins are naturally inquisitive about humans. Therefore, the two-legged critters in artificial coats would get as close to the penguins as they could then get still, often sitting or kneeling on the ground, camera in position. Eventually, if they were lucky, a curious penguin would advance near enough for someone to get a great photo and even better memory.

JP continued on past the hut and saw more penguins up ahead. Remembering that the Hut Point Ridge Trail offered an overlook of that area, he turned toward the trailhead and wound around until he was looking down at a large number of penguins and only a couple of people.

Once he was settled, his feet planted in a wide and stable stance, JP started shooting photos and video with his camera. The wind was remarkably calm and the "ack-ack" sound of the Adelies was crystal clear. At least, JP decided to go with "ack-ack" as nothing else seemed to provide as fit a description.

The couple in Big Reds were getting a great view. They were both on their knees with their backs to JP and the ridge, allowing the penguins to practically sniff them out.

After a good amount of coming and going by the birds, JP noticed a line of penguins moving with purpose from his left. He switched his camera back to video mode and started filming the eight penguins as they waddled in a form of follow the leader, weaving between other birds.

An Adelie's walking style – short-legged, rapid steps with flippers extended for balance – is always entertaining video, all the more when you have eight of them in single file. JP concentrated on keeping the group framed as it crossed just below him, running by the two humans in red.

Suddenly, the leader plunged into a small hole in the ice and its seven followers did the same without breaking stride. JP managed to not comment so as to not mess up his video, but then he heard a somewhat familiar voice pipe up from down below.

"Look, he just did a Peltzer."

By the time JP moved the camera toward the two he decided the voice belonged to Jackson Merkel, the GASP grad student. As they came into his viewfinder, he saw one of them slap the other on the back of the parka hood.

"Be quiet, you idiot," he heard in what he was sure was the voice of Chris Begin, the researcher.

Neither of them turned around and JP decided it would be best if he slipped behind the ridge before they did.

NOVEMBER 15, 7:10 A.M.

After a fitful night trying to sleep, JP got up early, put a load of laundry into a washer, ate breakfast and was sitting at his desk in the Sun office waiting for the clothes to finish drying.

He had uploaded the penguin photos and videos to his laptop in the room and transferred the last video to a flash drive, which was now plugged into his work computer.

Wearing headphones so he could crank up the sound, JP played the end of the video several times.

He just did a Peltzer; there's no doubt that's what he said, JP thought, his left thumb and forefinger massaging his chin. It's almost confirmed by the reaction it got. And I'm even more certain those were Begin and Merkel.

"But what does it mean?" he finally said out loud, just as Marcellus Stapler stuck his head in the doorway.

"Good morning, JP. I'm off to my last galley-cooked breakfast for the next few weeks. Care to join me?"

The reporter clumsily removed his earphones while closing the program and rapidly replaying in his mind his spoken words, reassuring himself he had not said anything out loud that might tip his hand.

"I'm sorry, I had my headphones on," he said, realizing he wasn't acting normal. "Uh, did you say breakfast?"

"Indeed. We're flying out later this morning. Everyone else ate early and they're now packing. I opted to pack first. Have you eaten?"

"Uh, no, I mean, yes, I've eaten breakfast and no, I can't really join you. I need to remove laundry from the dryer before someone does it for me and then I have a lot to work through here. But, listen, you have a safe trip and good luck with your research. People seem to redeploy quickly, but don't you go home without seeing me."

JP hoped a firm handshake removed any suspicions but also considered Stapler really had nothing to be suspicious about. He didn't know what was said or that JP heard it. Besides, the exchange could have been nothing more than Merkel exhibiting poor taste and Begin disciplining him.

And, even if the two did kill Peltzer, that didn't

implicate Stapler. Or did it?

"I wonder how easily you could quietly commit murder among a close-knit, eight-member group working together in a trans-Antarctic traverse," JP mumbled once he had shut the door and resumed sitting, this time staring at his computer's background image.

"Peltzer's disappearance was investigated and they obviously found no red flags or, at the very least, they wouldn't have let the team return." He was talking in a whisper now, something he tended to do when processing complicated or confusing information.

"The SAR team would have done everything possible to find Peltzer and the NSF would want to make sure nothing amiss would soil the program. Of course, maybe they wouldn't want to find something wrong. This is silly; surely my tingling reporter's radar is off on this one."

He sat silently for a minute until the computer's screen saver came on. JP shook his head and said out loud, "Bubba, I think I could use your help here. Oh, got to get my laundry and then insert a penguin reference in my column and e-mail it."

NOVEMBER 18, 4:44 P.M.

Juan Mendoza was in the zone, pumping out paperwork required of him in his job with Oldport County Animal Control Department, when co-worker Alexa walked in, tossing a copy of the Odds and Ends newspaper on the side of his desk.

"Isn't this your friend who adopted that ferret? I think you'll enjoy his article."

Juan leaned back in his chair and started reading.

By JP WEISCARVER
Oldport Odds and Ends
It was drilled into us during orientation. It was reinforced upon arrival. There are occasional reminders

still. When you're in Antarctica, you may not get too close to the animals. You may approach them, you're certainly encouraged to take photographs, but do not get too close.

Luckily, they define too close. If the animal – and that is likely a penguin or a seal – reacts to your presence, then you're too close.

That's all part of the Antarctic Treaty. When we come here, we agree to abide by it. Mess with a penguin and you may find yourself on the next plane out of here. You might even face charges.

We had our first penguin appearance this week and I found that everyone behaved themselves ... the people, that is. It helps that the penguins so readily approach people.

But back to the story of one of the neatest experiences for me so far.

While the folks in charge are strict about not approaching wildlife, scientists, of course, have a system for getting permission to do so. Research demands that they approach and often handle the animals and that is understood. And that is where my good luck came in.

They call it a morale trip. Supposedly, I was nominated for a job well done. I think someone felt sorry for me. Regardless, I got the chance to accompany a group of scientists while they were studying Weddell seals.

Yep, I got close enough to seals that they reacted to my presence ... and it was OK.

When we first started out, the lead scientist checked for an e-mail to see if one of the seals he wanted to find today had surfaced. Transmitters on these animals would send a signal somewhere that would be relayed someplace and within a few minutes of surfacing, an e-mail goes out.

"Good news," we heard him say. "Roxanne is out around Big Razorback Island."

Roxanne was their primary objective on this day. She was the first animal they placed monitors on two weeks earlier. Today was the first day they could retrieve their equipment and start analyzing data.

Five researchers and four visitors, including me, set out for a drive across the sea ice that covers McMurdo Sound, following the flagged route that marked a safe course. Eventually, we turned toward the volcano Mount Erebus and approached Big Razorback. Gradually, dark spots took form around the ice perimeter of the island. Actually, form is not the best way to put it. Seals lounging on the ice, which is about all any of them were doing, are little more than blobs. They were merely smoother than any volcanic rock outcroppings.

The faster part of our group had already located Roxanne and we moved the vehicles to that area, keeping all but the one carrying equipment well away from the seals. Two of the researchers "herded" the seal, a 10-year-old female who did not give birth this spring, to an area where they sedated her. Slowly, patiently, they removed the monitors and took blood and tissue samples, constantly keeping an eye on Roxanne's breathing until she came out from under the anesthesia.

That was neat but not my really fun part.

A couple of the scientists returned to town with the samples and data. The rest of us headed to Tent Island. Our objective was to track down some more seals that filled the needs for the research project. All we did was carefully approach the seals one at a time, leaving alone nursing pups and their mommas, and record the tag numbers on their tail flippers.

Here, I got close enough that the seals reacted to my presence. There wasn't much reaction from the majority of them, I'll admit, though a few were worked up and didn't want to show us their tags. But the point was that we were walking among them, authorized by permits to do so.

Traveling to the Ice is a rarity, but walking among seals in Antarctica is almost unheard of.

That's what I got to do and it was cool.

"Yep, that's my JP," Juan said as he refolded the paper.

"At least we know he won't be adopting any seals or penguins."

NOVEMBER 19, 6:12 P.M.

JP wanted a little quiet time during dinner, so he grabbed the most out-of-the-way two-person table he could find and then sat with his back to the room. The food was fine, not that he really paid much attention, though the dessert was a peach cobbler that almost brought him out of his meditation.

Almost.

What do I know that should cause a reasonable person to think there was foul play with Shane Peltzer's disappearance? Stapler told me before I left Oldport that Peltzer was an odd duck and nobody liked him, but that's not uncommon enough to be suspicious.

Jennifer was all levels of concerned but couldn't say why. Family and friends couldn't believe he would have committed suicide or that he was dumb enough to make a deadly mistake. However, I know from Happy Camp that extreme cold can really cloud up one's thinking. Nothing near conclusive there.

Then, I overhear one of his teammates make a rude comment mimicking Peltzer's death. That's not illegal, not even an indictment. Sure, Begin shushed Merkel, but that more likely meant he was tired of his tasteless humor than that he was covering up a murder.

What do I know? Nothing of substance.

But there's my gut. I've always respected my reporter's nose and it's served me well. Of course, Jennifer was saying the same thing. Did she influence my feelings? That's possible, I guess.

I'm not getting anywhere, am I? Guess I'll just keep my eyes open and look for an opportunity to learn something else.

With that, he gathered his dishes and trash on his tray

and headed toward the dish drop. As JP rounded the corner, he saw Brian Embers coming toward him.

"This cannot be a coincidence," the reporter mumbled under his breath.

JP dragged his feet just a bit in the dish drop. There were receptacles there in which diners scrape their food scraps and another to receive trash. Next, tableware was to be divided by the type of utensil in bins and glasses emptied and placed upside down in a holder for the dishwasher.

Trays were placed in a stack and plates handed straight to a dining attendant who would quickly rinse and stack them in another holder.

It normally took just a couple of seconds, but JP managed to allow Brian to catch up by the time he exited the dish drop toward the entrance hall.

"Hey, Brian, how's it going?" JP said once they were clear of the dining hall area. He detected Brian's uncertainty in his reply. "My name's JP Weiscarver; I was one of your Happy Campers at the beginning of the season."

"Yeah, yeah, I remember. You're the reporter dude and it was that really miserable class."

"That's the one," JP said as they shook hands. "Listen, I never appropriately thanked you for talking me down that day. It was about to get to me, but you did a great job of getting me settled."

"Hey, I only blabbered, you worked it out."

"Would you like to take a walk around the station, get a little fresh air?" JP asked. "I have something I'd like to talk to you about."

"Sure, sure. I want to hit up the ship's store while it's open and get a six-pack. We can drop it by my dorm as we start out."

NOVEMBER 19, 6:48 P.M.

"OK, Lord, if I'm onto something, please lead my research," JP said softly while walking around outside Building 207, one of the so-called Upper Case Dorms, in which each room housed two people and each pair of rooms shared a rest room.

He was pumping his arms to keep warm when Brian exited.

"That was quick," JP said, as they started walking toward the sea ice. "Oh, I usually walk a loop this way, turning left at the chapel, going behind Crary toward Berg and the fuel storage tanks and then taking the Scott Base road back into town."

"Sounds like a plan. Let's do it."

They traded small talk for a while. JP learned Brian lived in Hawaii.

"Wow, that's some transition, isn't it?" the reporter asked.

"No more so than coming from the Gulf of Mexico. Summers are hotter there than in Hilo."

"Oh, you're from the Big Island. Cool. I really want to visit sometime. It seems like one amazingly diverse place. What is it, all but one or two ecological types?"

"At the risk of sounding like I'm reciting it from memory, which I am, 'There are supposedly 13 climactic regions on the planet and the Big Island has 11, all but Arctic and Saharan.' You know, JP, you can have USAP book your return flight with a layover in Hawaii. You just pay the difference between that and a straight flight home; there's no cheaper way to get there without joining the Navy."

"Yeah, I've heard such stories. We'll see how things shake out the next couple of months."

As they neared the drive to the Carpentry Workshop, JP felt comfortable enough to broach his topic.

"There's a reason I dragged you out here. You know I'm a reporter, not just for the Sun but in the 'real world,' and one thing a good reporter hopes to develop is a sense of when something's not right. I've felt particularly blessed in that regard and have a lot of personal respect for those feelings."

JP glanced at Brian in an attempt to gauge his grasp of what he was trying to say and felt he saw an understanding.

"I've had something nibbling at me, something about which I have absolutely no concrete evidence and, well, I'd like to see if you've had some concerns, too, or if maybe you can put my mind at ease."

"OK, you're killing me here," Brian said, stopping alongside the road on the downhill approach to town.

"You were here last year, so you know about the Shane Peltzer disappearance."

"Very well. I was on the SAR team that looked for him."

"Oh, is it permissible for you to talk about it?"

"Sure, it's not like I'm a criminal investigator or anything. Is there something in particular you want to know?"

JP shrugged. They were walking again, though slowly.

"Truth is, I don't know anything about particulars," he finally said. "Something just doesn't feel right about it. Did you find anything strange?"

"Strangeness is relative on the Ice," Brian said after a moment's thought, drawing a nod from JP. "Thankfully, I don't have anything else to compare it to as far as a search-and-rescue operation, so I'm not really in a position to say whether the GASP mission was any stranger.

"That being said ... Hey, Luke, how's it going?" Brian interrupted himself when they met someone carrying a package from the MCC. "That being said, everything seemed strange to me. Everyone said Peltzer had been moody but such was his normal state. It seemed only a couple of people had seen him recently; most weren't too sure but said it was normal to not take note of his presence because he did not interact with others. He often took his food to eat alone and he slept in his own compartment in the workshop module."

"You're sounding a bit like me but better informed," JP said. "Things just don't quite add up to normal."

"As a rescue guy, though, what we found there was what was strangest. Rather, perhaps, what we didn't find."

JP waited while Brian organized his thoughts.

"I really haven't considered all of this in a while, I guess," he finally said. "Perhaps that was on purpose."

"Do you think someone killed him?"

"No, no. I mean, there's no reason to think so. What I found most strange was there was no apparent threat. The weather was good, the equipment working and all in a known-to-be-safe area. They essentially said they just looked up and found Peltzer was not there."

"If he was such a social malcontent, is it possible he just flipped out and went for long, suicidal walk?"

"Actually, that's about the only thing that fits. You want to do another lap?"

"If you don't mind. So, the GASP team searched for him and then called for help?"

"Actually, I believe they called us as soon as they realized he was not there and then began their search while we organized at this end."

"Did you do a helicopter search?"

"They were too far out for us to get choppers there," Brian said. "We flew out on an LC-130 after they assured us there was a good landing area. Before landing, we flew six circles around a broad area looking for clues. The view from there isn't perfect, but we had every set of eyes looking. All we spotted were three suspicious areas that all proved to be natural formations."

"You said the weather was clear, so there should have been tracks, right?"

"Well, weather was clear but it's out on the open ice and there's always wind. Nothing like we experienced in your Happy Camp but enough to cover tracks rather quickly, certainly long before we arrived."

"I was told you stayed in the area for a couple of days."

"Yes. After the Air National Guard crew dropped us off, they did more of a grid search before returning. We pitched camp and worked the area as well as we could for two days. On the morning of the third day, another flight picked us up and returned us home."

"And GASP continued to its destination?"

"Yes. Actually, they left the second day we were there. They were in a tremendous time crunch and all of this slowed them down quite a bit. We stayed on another day before leaving."

"How did you search any crevasses in the area?" JP asked. "Do you have some sort of equipment for it?"

"That's what I was talking about earlier when I said it was an area with a reputation for being safe. There are no known crevasses for probably 50 miles and we didn't find anything that looked like a threat."

"So, Shane Peltzer just walked off and buried himself in the snow."

"That's more or less our best guess, JP. And while it's not something I'm happy with, I haven't heard anything more plausible. Sometimes, you just chalk it up to the fact strange things happen on the Ice."

NOVEMBER 24, 11:34 P.M.

"Hello, JP" Jennifer answered the phone.

"How did you know it was me?"

"You always have the same toll-free number showing on the caller ID, silly boy. But I am confused by one thing. I'm thinking about dinner here, so doesn't that mean it's awfully late where you are?"

"Yeah, it's 11:30 here. I, uh, wanted to try and make sure we weren't interrupted, so I came down to the office at a time it's unlikely either of my partners walks in."

"How sweet."

"Right, that's it. Anyway, should I change the topic

suddenly or end the call unfinished, we'll resume later."

"Positively clandestine and I love it. Please tell me it's about Shane Peltzer."

"It's not easy here, Jennifer. I mean, there is no Open Records Act, nor an accessible law enforcement report. It's worse because I'm not in a watchdog situation. The newspaper here is an arm of the establishment. That's mostly OK for writing about the things I'm supposed to cover, but it's difficult to investigate a murder."

"He was murdered?"

"Sorry, that was misleading. I actually have only uneasy thoughts and unanswered questions."

"Run them by me."

He gave her a fairly thorough synopsis of his conversation with Brian Embers, complete enough to communicate his mounting exasperation.

"I understand your frustration," she said, "but it's hard to get too worked up when there's no body, no smoking gun, no red flag."

"Well, there is one thing that's really worked on my conscience. I told you about the penguins several days ago, but I didn't mention what I heard. Remember the part about the line of birds flopping into a hole in the ice?"

"Yeah, and I loved your photos, by the way."

"You can tell by the photos that I was on a ridge above them. Below me, with me out of their line of sight, were two guys off the GASP team. When the lead bird went in, one of them said, 'Look, he just did a Peltzer.'"

"Ouch, but seriously, JP, that could just be an idiot talking."

"For sure and that's what I had just about written it off to, but then Brian's information made me look at it in a different way. Merkel – that's his name – made reference to Peltzer as if he fell through the ice, as if he knew what happened to him. But Brian pretty much ruled out any such incident. They know of no crevasses in the area and found no further evidence of any. So, why did Merkel think the stumbling penguin resembled Peltzer?"

NOVEMBER 27, 1:50 P.M.

"Congratulations, JP," Simon called out while reading through his e-mail. "Transport and lodging have been approved."

"Huh?" JP asked, pulled from his earphones while transcribing notes from an interview. "Oh, Pole?"

"Yes, sir, Mr. Weiscarver, it looks as if you're going to the South Pole."

"Cool! When?"

"You're scheduled for a 10 a.m. cargo flight on Dec. 10. You'll enjoy four nights at the luxurious Amundsen-Scott South Pole Station with such amenities as an unlimited view of the horizon, oxygen deprivation and altitude sickness induced by flying from sea level to more than 9,000 feet, and, most importantly, the opportunity to get your 'hero shot' standing next to a candy cane-striped pole."

"Not to mention," added JP, now standing at Simon's shoulder, "an overnight trip off station to take a look at Dr. Garret Farley's project. I'll get an e-mail off to him now; he's said he only needs to know when and that he's otherwise all-in for my visit."

"Since his project is built around drilling holes in the ice, you might be wary of going 'all-in.'"

NOVEMBER 28, 2:28 P.M.

The Antarctic Sun, while not a real newspaper by many standards, did cling to one aging feature. It was still printed.

The stories written by the journalism trio and other contributors became available to worldwide readers through the Internet. They were not only posted on the U.S. Antarctic Program's Web site but many unrelated science sites and even goofy pages would link to or downright take the stories.

In addition to that, once the stories had been edited and approved by numerous people, Simon and his crew laid them out with photos in a newspaper format designed to fit on standard copy paper. Following another round of proofing from the team and several volunteer readers around the station, printing was turned over to a large copy machine. The journalists took turns printing, collating and stapling a couple of hundred copies each week.

The copies went into a couple of racks and were spread around the galley. The hope was people would read and pass it on to someone else to minimize the number of copies needed each week.

Additionally, they stuffed varying numbers of the papers into manila envelopes to be distributed around the continent. Every week, copies traveled down the road to Scott Base and were flown to the South Pole. More impressive to JP was that they were also delivered to the various research camps along with their supply shipments.

For the journalists, the responsibilities of circulation ended with sticking the papers into envelopes and setting them aside for a courier.

There were two couriers who worked the station like tag team wrestlers. One worked with the Postal Service employee sorting incoming mail and passing out packages to people. The other spent most of the day moving around station, driving a pickup and moving in and out of buildings shuffling mail and office paperwork between locations. Each week, the couriers traded jobs.

They actually delivered the paper to Scott Base but the others they passed on to be flown by cargo plane or helicopter to the various field camps

"The Sun also rises," exclaimed Leslie, a line the courier found funny and insisted up using every time she entered the tiny office.

"Are your papers all here and ready to go?" she asked,

picking up the numerous envelopes.

"I believe so, Leslie," said Simon. "You take care of those; we worked particularly hard on them this week."

"It would shock me to the core if you ever did otherwise," she said. "JP, have you checked the package list? I believe something arrived for you this morning."

"Thanks, Leslie. No, I've not looked because I'm not expecting anything."

"That's the best kind. You folks have a great day."

NOVEMBER 28, 2:41 P.M.

JP immediately visited Leslie's partner in the package room at the MCC and returned with a box emblazoned with the logo of a popular brand of liquor.

"Wow, you have good connections back home, JP," Alexia said as he sat the box on his desk.

"Yeah, I had to listen to such comments all the way back. However, seeing the name on the return address, I can assure you the box is misleading."

Inside was a large envelope containing numerous layers of paper. He picked it up and saw underneath a plastic container full of an assortment of cookies. As he was extracting the treats, he realized there was a workmate on each shoulder.

"Have I told you, JP, that you're my favorite staff member?" Simon asked.

"Have I told you, JP, that I've written the president and suggested he make you lead journalist?" Alexia countered.

"Guys, guys, do you really think I would cut you out of the goodies?"

The other two looked at each other and shrugged. JP removed a chocolate chip cookie, examined it closely and said, just before putting it into his mouth, "Enjoy, my friends."

With the others chronicling the contents of the cookie shipment, JP opened the envelope. It was filled with numerous clippings from the Oldport Odds and Ends, topped by a letter from Lydia Murray.

"Dear JP, thanks for the nice words in your e-mail from New Zealand. I've never received a message from anyone in New Zealand before. If fact, I've never received anything from the Southern Hemisphere. What you're doing is so exciting and it's been fun following along with your columns.

"When Mom heard I was writing you, she insisted I send along some of her cookies. I know they're great and you like them, but I wasn't sure they would hold up to such a long journey. I hope so.

"Besides just saying hi, I also wanted to send you some clippings. There are a lot about hurricane recovery. JP, you are lucky to miss so much of this. Everyone stayed tough for a while, but eventually you just want things to be back to normal. On the good side, we should be in our office by the first of the year. On the questionable side, I found out that awful brown chair you kept by your desk made it through the storm. I overheard something about throwing it away, but I insisted they save it for you.

"You'll also see stories about criminal charges and lawsuits related to the hurricane. There's more ugliness than just leveled buildings, but I don't want to talk about that now.

"Other articles are some of the things I've done. I miss not asking your advice, but maybe it's making me more critical of my work instead of relying on you to do that for me. Anyway, I'd still welcome any thoughts or tips.

"Pat was sick last week, so I took over part of her load in Lifestyles. It was fulfilling having more responsibility, but I really don't want to do that full time. Thanks, again, for helping me get to the news side. Respectfully, Lydia."

Simon and Alexia had quietly returned to work while JP read the letter and shuffled through the clippings, most of which he had already read online.

"Who's our benefactor?" Simon asked.

"Huh?"

"Who sent the cookies, JP?" Alexia translated.

"Maxine Murray. She's the mother of a great young reporter in Oldport."

"Yeah?" Simon asked. He knew there was more of a story behind the statement.

"Yeah, her daughter Lydia had everything stacked against her but worked hard to force her way into the news room. She has no formal training, but she's shown a natural knack for ferreting out news."

"Guess that means she'll be moving on to big media soon," Simon added.

"No, I don't think so. I don't see her ever leaving Oldport. She'll more likely take over my job and eventually the city editor's job, if she wants them."

He then got down to clippings about criminal charges related to deaths and injuries during Hurricane Clarice and he thought about the role Lydia played and the risks she took in bringing those stories to light.

"Sometimes journalists forget they have an uncomfortable job," he continued, half to himself. "It's not about making friends and developing fans. Often, it's about finding a wrong and bringing it to light."

DECEMBER 2, 12:33 P.M.

"Hey, Mom, I forgot to tell you there's a JP column in the paper this morning," Lydia Murray yelled through the house. "I think you'll particularly enjoy this one. I left it on the coffee table for you."

Maxine plopped down and began reading, sometimes out loud, sometimes to herself.

By JP WEISCARVER
Oldport Odds and Ends
It doesn't take long to figure out everything is different in Antarctica.

Cold is colder, warm is cooler and distances are an illusion. Indeed, so many things we take for granted back home are life-sustaining essentials here, like running water.

In Oldport, little thought is given to a decision to hop in the car and drive to Queensland for dinner. Here, the only reasonable comparison would be walking or catching the shuttle for a Thursday night meal at neighboring Scott Base. Traveling beyond that requires securing hard-to-get permission and hitching a ride on a plane or helicopter.

So, it's no surprise holidays are different. For example, Thanksgiving comes on Saturday.

Before you get all up in arms about that piece of seeming sacrilege, let me explain why it is so and why everyone here loves it.

In such a setting, where people have limited responsibilities beyond work, it's a good idea to keep them busy. So, to help us stay out of trouble, our employer does three things.

The most time-honored maneuver is a heavy-handed threat to pack us up and send us home, without an end-of-the-season bonus, for causing too much trouble. Another thing is providing a lot of activities to fill leisure time, everything from cross-country snow skiing to knitting.

Top of the list, though, is we work long hours. Everyone here is expected to work six days a week, nine hours a day. Folks in my department usually work longer and that may be true of a lot of places. "At least you're racking up the overtime," you're probably thinking, but that's not the case. Since we're not "in" the United States, we're not protected by wage laws. That is, there is no overtime.

That's OK with most people; it's a tradeoff for the awesome experience.

Back to Thanksgiving.

Most of us work a Monday-Saturday week and are off on Sundays. You see where this is going now, don't you?

Celebrating Thanksgiving on Saturday means we get a

two-day weekend! And, in case you're wondering, the same practice is applied to Christmas. It will be observed on Saturday or Monday.

There's something else different here about Thanksgiving.

Back home, there's usually a big turkey and dressing meal with "all the trimmings." Maybe it's a ham or lobster or steak. Here, we had them all ... and so much more.

Knowing that we're all far from home during the holiday, they go all out in an effort to make it special. I'd say it was a total hit.

"That's kinda sweet, ain't it?" Maxine called out. "Did he get the cookies I made him?"

"Yes, I told you three days ago that he e-mailed me that he and his friends thoroughly enjoyed them," Lydia said entering the room. He said something else that sounded kinda funny. He said I was an inspiration to him to not forget his role as a reporter."

5 90 DEGREES SOUTH

"That should do it," JP murmured, standing in his dorm room looking at one of the orange flight bags issued him when he deployed.

"I have enough clothes, not that I need much for four days. I have my personal camera and the work camera. There's an extra note pad and pen, as well as a mechanical pencil if it's too cold at Farley's camp for ink to flow. I cannot believe I just said that."

"Do you always talk to yourself when packing for a trip?" asked Dwight Mooney.

"Only when my day-sleeping roommate is already awake. But, yeah, I do a lot of processing out loud. I kind of thought it was normal. Are you saying there's something wrong with me?"

"No, never. Speaking of things medical, did you get anything for altitude sickness? One of my roommates last year spent two weeks at Pole and he said it took him half that time to get used to the altitude."

"I was advised to do that and I picked up some Diamox from the clinic yesterday and started taking it this morning. They said it should help minimize symptoms."

"I guess you're pumped."

"Definitely. Going to Pole has its own category at the top of my Antarctic wish list. Then, the opportunity to visit a research camp is intimidatingly awesome. Did you get to go to Pole last year?"

"Are you kidding? Entry-level mechanics don't get to go to Pole just for the fun of it. Actually, toward the end of the season, if supply runs are going well and they have space, they'll sometimes take a few people at a time on morale trips. You fly three hours in an anything-but-comfortable jump seat in the belly of an LC-130, you run around at Pole while they offload fuel and cargo, then you fly back. It's a lot to put up with for a hero shot, but I'll put in for it this year. I mean, who gets to go to the South Pole?"

"Exactly. I'm ready."

DECEMBER 10, 1:14 P.M.

The comfort of flying in an LC-130 was somewhat overstated, JP had decided by the time the ski-equipped cargo plane touched down on the ice runway at the South Pole.

Worse than the seats, though, was the boredom. There were only two other passengers, neither of whom he knew, though he had seen one around station. Regardless, communicating was next to impossible because of the noise. All three wore either ear plugs or listened to music. Early in the flight, one of them made the other two aware they were crossing the Transantarctic Mountains and all peeked out the small windows.

But all were alert after the crew member informed them to buckle up in preparation to land. There was no waiting once the plane was on the ground. As soon as JP had his layers of clothing secured and his bag in hand, he was ushered to the door.

He wasn't sure what he was expecting, but what he found was a madhouse of activity. After hours of near-solitude, he looked out at numerous heavily-clothed figures moving hoses, driving fork lifts, taking care of any number of details he could not guess.

When he descended the steps to the ice, a stream of air blasted him from the plane's propellers. That accentuated the temperature, which he was told before landing was minus 17 degrees.

At the bottom of the steps, just like when he landed at McMurdo, were people to make sure he went the right way or, more specifically, that he did not go the wrong way. In the confusion, he noticed someone hurrying toward him.

"JP!" she yelled above the din as she threw her arms around him. "Welcome to the South Pole."

"Cindy Murphy, I wasn't expecting you to greet me."

"Silly boy, I'm a fuelie, remember? Part of my job is to offload this fuel into our storage tank, which I need to do now. I'll catch you later."

JP and his two traveling partners were directed toward the elevated station and told to take the exterior stairway to the second floor, where they were expected.

This is all happening too fast, JP thought as he trudged toward the structure, all the while trying to take in his surroundings. He turned at one point to look at the activity surrounding the aircraft. A forklift on large snow tires was exiting the rear ramp door with a crate in its grasp. Hoses were drawing excess fuel from the plane's tanks. JP knew that was one of the functions of the flights. The planes were rigged to carry more fuel than the trip required, so the excess was deposited at the station, slowly building up fuel supplies needed to make it through the long winter.

He turned back toward the station. Off to his left he could see the vastness opening up, though there were various structures for different major research programs. To his right, behind the elevated station, was a hodgepodge of small buildings and storage areas.

The station itself sat on 36 huge columns that held the building well above the surface to allow snow to blow underneath. As the ice builds higher – the area already sat on ice about 9,000 feet thick – the columns can be extended as much as 24 feet.

It was during the walk to the station, which seemed much farther than it looked, he finally started feeling the cold seep through. That's OK, he thought, he had more layers to put on before going out for an extended stay.

Finally, they arrived at the stairs and started climbing. The station sat about 50 feet above the ground and they were going to the second floor. As he worked his way up the stairs, JP realized he was breathing heavily. He had heard the apparent altitude at Pole is actually much higher than the actual altitude and he was feeling that in his lungs.

Once the three travelers worked through the double entryway, they were greeted by Jo Sparks, South Pole station manager. After showing them where to hang their parkas and drop their bags, she led them into a conference room.

JP knew what was next. It did not take long to learn nothing happens on the Ice without an orientation.

Jo made quick and pleasant work of passing on the required information and underscoring many of the same safety reminders.

"You're all residents of Mac Town," she said, "so there are a couple of things in particular with which you might not be familiar.

"First, we do not have the huge janitor staff you're accustomed to having clean up behind you. Here, we have house mouse duties. You will clean your area. Additionally, there is a chart on the inside of your berth that will tell you the day of the week for which you're responsible for helping clean the rest room. You're each here for a brief time, but should you be here on the assigned day, you're a house mouse.

"Finally, we are incredibly stingy with our water here

because it is so difficult to come by. Therefore, everyone at Pole is limited to one two-minute shower a week. That doesn't concern you because you won't be here long enough to need a shower."

With that, she handed each an envelope that had a station map, a berth assignment and a beautiful certificate noting the recipient's achievement of visiting the South Pole.

"What about our room key?" asked one of JP's co-travelers.

"Oh, I forgot to mention that. Our berths here do not have locks. Theft has never been a problem, perhaps because we're such a close community and perhaps because there's nowhere to run."

DECEMBER 10, 3:12 P.M.

JP found his room in wing A4 and immediately understood why they were called "berths" instead of "rooms."

It measured only 9 feet by 7 feet. There was a small closet. Additional storage was available underneath a bed that was almost too high off the floor. In the corner was a built-in desk with a chair.

"Only a toilet shy of being up to prison standards," he said. "But, hey, I have the room to myself."

It took only a minute to get settled in and JP set out on a tour of the building, stopping first at the rest room, where he found the waterless fixtures, as advertised.

He began at the far end of the building by stepping out of the door into what the locals called the beer can. While the stairway he took to enter the station was on the outside, its complementing feature on the other end was enclosed in a huge, round metal structure that looked like a can. It was not heated and, though it was not nearly as cold as outside, he did not hang around for long.

Re-entering the main building, he took a right and

looped through the galley, where a few people were hanging out having coffee or a snack. He knew it would be smaller but was still surprised by how small it was.

Passing by the dish drop and some recycling bins, he completed a circle back to the primary hallway and ventured on. There were lockers along the wall, much like he remembered from high school. Some of them had firefighter bunker gear positioned for use in case of an alarm.

Continuing down the hall, he passed the biomedical unit and a computer room before walking through a connecting walkway that offered flexibility between the two segments of the station to help counter ice movement.

On his left was a game room with televisions to watch recorded programming, since there was no live TV. To the right, he passed doorways into some science labs before coming upon a collection of offices and the meeting room where he had orientation.

Having reached the end, he turned down the interior stairway, which began with an overlook into the gymnasium below, which he stole a look into once he got downstairs. Heading to the first floor hallway, he passed an activity room that housed a small collection of musical instruments.

Proceeding up the hall, past the cloakroom, was the communications room. Next were utility rooms, recycling room and an arts and crafts room before passing through the connecting walkway.

He took a look into the reading room, where he found a few copies of The Antarctic Sun lying on the table. Passing by the laundry room, he peered through a glass wall into the greenhouse. In addition to being an uplifting sight for people who have gone months without seeing any green plants, this small room helped give the station a supply of fresh salad, cucumbers and tomatoes, particularly important during the eight-month winter lockdown.

Rounding out his tour, he stepped into the station

store. Behind the counter was Jo Sparks.

"Wow, you must do everything here," JP said to the station manager, who had just handed an employee a package that had come in the mail.

"You just read my job description," she said. "Underneath 'station manager,' it says, 'Do everything.' Did you find your berth all right?"

"Oh, yes, and I'm completing a survey of the station and I figured this was a good time to pick out a souvenir."

"Here's my favorite," she said, handing him a beer stein. He tilted it and looked inside: "I reached the bottom at the South Pole."

"I'll take it."

DECEMBER 10, 5:44 P.M.

A tray of food in front of him, JP picked a spot in the galley that offered an expansive view of ice and snow, letting his imagination wander a bit while enjoying his meal.

He was also watching for Cindy Murphy, the one person at Pole he already knew. Actually, he didn't know her all that well. She hung out with Alexia in the Sun office a lot while waiting for weather at the Pole to allow flights. A bubbly personality, she was someone fun to hang around with.

"Hey, there, newbie, how you doing?" she said, having sneaked up on him.

"I'm great, Cindy. Join me. Actually, I just lied to you; I'm not all that great. When do I catch my breath? Climbing a flight of stairs knocks me out."

"You're here for four days, so I'd say you'll be fine shortly after touching down back at McMurdo."

"I thought those anti-altitude sickness drugs was supposed to help me handle it."

"I'm no doctor or anything, but I believe that's more for keeping you from losing this wonderful meal. It doesn't exactly put more oxygen into your bloodstream. What do you have planned while visiting us?"

"My real work begins tomorrow. I'm to meet someone from Garret Farley's team for lunch and then we're headed to their camp for a day. Before and after that, I'm taking some photos to go with stories we're running later and I'm interviewing a cook for a profile."

"Farley, huh? That will be fun. Sounds like this evening is as good a time as any for us to get your picture made next to the South Pole. You game?"

"You know I am. I was hoping you would do me the honor."

After dinner, JP and Cindy each ran to their berths for cameras and reconvened at the beer can door. He followed her lead about how tightly to bundle up before entering the can. They chatted while walking down, their voices echoing somewhat before submitting to the noise generated by the wind. At the bottom, they completed securing their clothing and exited.

"I checked just before we started down and the temperature has dropped to minus 19," Cindy said.

"And we're less than two weeks from the beginning of summer," JP replied, trying to speak clearly through his face covering.

"How cold does it get where you come from?" she asked.

"I've been there five years now and it's dropped below freezing a couple of times. Where I grew up, we'd drop below zero for brief times, but nothing like this. What about you?"

"I'm from Colorado and we'd get pretty cold during the winter, but summer was fantastic. Your summers are too hot, in my opinion."

"Understood, but Oldport does get nice cooling breezes off the Gulf of Mexico."

"Yeah, but sometimes those breezes earn names."

"Clarice was no fun, that's for sure, but you have

tradeoffs wherever you are."

"Speaking of where we are, you move over here next to this pole and I'll take your photo while you contemplate the fact that every person on Earth is due north of you."

After taking a couple of photos with JP's camera, Cindy took one with her own, explaining she was keeping a virtual scrapbook of all her Antarctic friends.

"I worked last summer at Glacier National Park and I just accepted a job next summer at Yellowstone," she explained. "I hope to get back down here next year at either McMurdo or Palmer. In other words, I foresee myself doing something like this as long as it's fun. Therefore, I need a way to keep up with all of my friends scattered around the world."

"Wow. You know, I'm incredibly happy with my life, but there is a certain allure to what you're doing."

"I know," she said, her smile obvious in her voice. "I'm living the dream."

Since the wind had died down considerably, they decided to take a walk before going back inside.

"I apologize for bringing up the temperature again," JP said. "It must get boring. But how cold was it earlier this season."

"Of course, they didn't even fly us in until a certain level of warmth was achieved, but we still had cold spells after I arrived. The coldest, though, was 72 degrees below zero."

"Ouch, and you worked in that?"

"No, I wasn't outside. There's less for me to do outside when the planes can't fly."

"Right, they don't let them land here when it's that cold."

"The official line of what they call functionality cutoffs are minus 40 degrees for machinery such as cranes, minus 50 degrees for aircraft and, get this, minus 80 degrees for people."

JP just shook his head.

"I have another question for you. Maybe it's something you've heard discussed. Let's say you're in full ECW, maybe with some water and a few snacks but without any gear, how long could a person expect to survive out here."

"At minus 72?"

"No, like we have now. What did you say? Minus 19?"

"Hmm, there are a lot of variables, I think, most of them being how the person handled it. He could last a pretty good while, especially if it was planned and there was an escape mechanism. If it was an accident, it would take a well-disciplined person to keep from freaking out and doing something stupid. With the ECW, you could withstand the cold for quite a while, plenty of time to dig a snow cave where you can conserve your body heat. But you're going to need food before long. Pretty soon, your body will run out of fat to burn and will start shutting down organs. Again, I'm no doctor, but I think you're talking about a few days, depending on how the person deals with it."

The reporter continued walking in silence.

"JP," Cindy said, grabbing his elbow. "I'm wondering why you're asking."

"Just thinking about something," he said, but he then more accurately read her body language. "Oh, don't worry. I'm not planning on going on a suicide trip. It was for another story I might be doing. As for me, I have to come see you in Yellowstone next summer."

DECEMBER 11, 11:24 A.M.

Every time someone walked by the door to the reading room, JP looked up. Unable to concentrate, he finally put down the two-year-old magazine and practiced patience, something at which he seldom excelled.

Finally, a man stepped into the doorway.

"I take it you're JP Weiscarver," he said. "I'm Garret Farley. Walk with me."

JP grabbed his bag and did as he was told. Farley was already talking as the reporter caught up with him and followed him up the center stairway.

"One of us comes into the station every day about this time to deliver a sample to the lab. The minions there perform tests for us, which are ready to pick up when we bring in the next day's sample. I don't like this to be indoors too long before handing it over," he said, raising a small container. "I really should have taken it up first, but that would mean climbing the stairs twice."

As they approached the lab door, Farley stopped, looked at JP and said, "Wait here."

Lunch with Farley wasn't any more entertaining. JP followed him – of course – through the food line and was tempted to keep up with the number of rude and self-serving comments the researcher made. When he chose a seat, JP took the chair opposite him, confident nobody else would approach. It's a small station, after all, and the reputation of someone like Farley would be well known.

All attempts to visit failed and JP resigned to simply eating. He was staring across the room when Cindy stepped into his line of sight, mouthing, "I'm sorry." JP smiled as he remembered her words the day before, "Farley, huh? That will be fun."

Anticipating a hasty departure, JP made sure to eat quickly, which was easy since there was no distracting conversation. Sure enough, Farley pushed away from the table and started rising from his chair as he asked, though it was obviously a command instead of a question, "You ready?"

DECEMBER 11, 1:57 P.M.

Riding on the back of an Alpine 2 snowmobile for more than 30 miles left JP stiff when he dismounted at the field camp. He started to speak to Farley, but the scientist was already moving away and yelling toward his assistants.

"I'm entering this new data. Clint, please take care of the snowmobile. Sara, please take care of our visitor."

His commands were unnecessary, JP noticed, because they were already doing just those things, during which introductions were made. As Sara showed him to a tent, he saw Clint preparing to fuel the snowmobile.

"You'll stay the night in here with Clint and the radio," Sara said. "You didn't bring a sleeping bag, did you?"

"No, Dr. Farley told me not to, that you had one."

"Just making sure. Actually, that was me on all those e-mails. He doesn't like to tend to communications but insists his name is on everything."

"That seems to fit the character," JP said, selecting his words slowly.

"You have the good doctor pegged already, it appears. Hang on, I need to check you in."

Sara had already turned on the radio and taken off her large, outer gloves to pick up the microphone.

"Scott Base, Scott Base, this is Delta Zulu One Five Two requesting relay to Mac Ops, over."

"Delta Zulu One Five Two, this is Scott Base. Good afternoon, Sara. Prepared to receive relay message, over."

"Hello, Rhianna. Doc has returned from his lab run and we're checking in safe and well with four souls today. We have an overnight visitor."

"What a lucky person that is. Do you have any weather observations for them? I am prepared to copy."

"Of course I do. Delta Zulu One Five Two is showing wind from 80 degrees at 10 knots, visibility six miles, clear skies, temperature minus 29, surface good, horizon good, over."

"Received, stand by."

Sara laid the microphone in her lap.

"Your first time in a field camp?" she asked and JP nodded, unsure about talking over the background noise of the radio. "You're probably aware we have to check in with Mac Ops every day. We do it now so we can also notify Pole that our rider is back from the run. McMurdo's weather geeks, bless their hearts, also request field camps to provide local readings to supplement what they get from satellites."

"Delta Zulu One Five Two, this is Scott Base. Mac Ops has received your transmission, thanks you for the boring weather report and Sunny says howdy to JP, over," to which JP flapped gloved fingers at the radio.

"JP sends an affirming wave and we'll talk to you in the morning as I leave to bring him back."

"So, you take turns making the run into Pole?"

"For the most part, though Doc sometimes skips a turn. Like that, we can each get a good, hot meal every two to three days. Plus, it doesn't hurt to get away from here."

"Tell me that he's better to work with on a professional level, that maybe he just doesn't have social skills," JP said.

"I could tell you that, if you want, but I'd rather not start our relationship with lies."

"Ouch, so why do it?"

"Well, you don't get too many choices to do post-doctoral work, he really is good at what he does and, most importantly, accepting this appointment gave me a chance to do field work in Antarctica, something that is tough to beat on a resume. But, Doc? There's no glossing over that he's a pain to deal with, but he's not mean, he carries a fair if not totally equitable share of the load and, last but not least, he has a solid reputation in our profession and gives an outstanding reference to those who have survived field work with him."

"Fair enough. Surely I can put up with him for 20-something hours."

"Don't worry about that," Sara said. "You will hardly see him again and there's no need to even talk to him. He put Clint and me in charge of showing you what we're doing and answering questions."

"I have a couple of questions right off, but they're not directly related to your research. You gave the wind as coming from 80 degrees. I understand that to be almost out of the east, but how do you determine east when you're basically on the polar axis? I mean, every direction is north."

"Good question," said Clint, who had just crawled into his tent. "We make it up."

"He's almost serious," Sara said. "You're right, JP, and that problem was understood long ago and someone developed a grid, placing zero degrees along the Greenwich Meridian. The grid lines run parallel and perpendicular to each other, rather than converging at the poles."

"So, you make it up," JP said. "I can handle that. Next one is trivial, perhaps. You tell them in your daily check-in how many people you have; does it change that often?"

"Not at all. In fact, you're our first and may be our last visitor. It's just something they have us do."

DECEMBER 17, 6:05 P.M.

"You can quit waving now, I'm here," JP said between laughs while taking a seat across the dinner table from Sunny DelSol.

"I was afraid, after your trip to Pole, your magnetic compass might be out of whack and you'd lose sight of me."

"Sunny, I don't think it's possible to lose sight of you. Whatever the environment, you're going to stand out."

"Aw, I bet you melted part of the polar ice cap with such sentiments. So, tell me, how was it?"

"That's one reason I e-mailed you a dinner invite," JP said. "I would like to get your honest feelings about this column before I send it off. Is it safe for you to read and eat?"

"As long as you don't mind should I get chicken juice on the printout."

By JP WEISCARVER
Oldport Odds and Ends

Ever since being accepted into the U.S. Antarctic Program, I have said I had one thing on my wish list while on the frozen continent.

Much could be on such a list, like seeing a penguin, camping on a glacial ice shelf, visiting the Dry Valleys, climbing a mountain, seeing a seal, skiing, learning about things from astronomy to marine biology, seeing a whale and riding in a helicopter.

Many of those things may be on my secondary list and some of them are checked off, but the only thing that I've had on my main wish list was to visit the South Pole.

Before proceeding, a geography refresher is in order. Many people think going to Antarctica automatically means going to the South Pole. Remember that the continent is larger than the United States and Mexico. McMurdo Station, where I work, is more than 800 miles from the South Pole, which is a single point somewhat centrally located on the continent.

Another note worth making is expressed on a T-shirt I've seen around: "Antarctica – It's Down." A lot of people hear Antarctica and think about the Arctic, up toward Santa Claus and the North Pole.

Truth is, while not many people get to Antarctica, far fewer still make the trip to the South Pole, which is one of the three full-time U.S. stations on the Ice. As a journalist, I knew I had a better chance than a lot of people stationed at McMurdo, but it was not a given, a fact driven home when a trip scheduled to coincide with a big anniversary observance in October was unceremoniously axed. "They" did not see any need for me to go.

The other two folks on our staff have made the trip to Pole in the past. So they offered to change the story distribution a bit to give me another crack at going.

And it worked. As I write this, I am sitting within a Tiger Woods tee shot of the actual South Pole.

119

One of my workmates e-mailed the question, "What do you think of the bottom of the world?"

What came to mind was a journal entry written by Sir Robert Falcon Scott, the Englishman who in the summer of 1911-12 lost the race to be the first man to 90 degrees south latitude. He and his party never made it back from the journey, but a search party found the journal with his body almost a year later.

His most remembered comment about the South Pole: "Great God, this is an awful place."

Don't get me wrong. I am forever thankful for the opportunity and the experience. Some things are worth seeing or doing even if they are discomforting. But, unlike the mother who "forgets" the pain of childbirth long enough to endure another, I imagine one trip to Pole will be enough for me.

Of course, I am not getting the opportunity to become acclimated, particularly to the two-mile-high altitude. High altitude sickness is a real threat since almost everyone arrives here by plane from sea level. I received drugs to help and I have been conscientious about drinking loads of water, but walking up a flight of stairs still winds me even after three days.

Earlier today, I all but ran out to get photos of an airdrop. It's maybe half a mile. I was puffing like a freight train. By the time I got back, my ribs were sore from labored breathing.

They do a lot to make life pleasant, though. Particularly nice for me was having a room to myself.

And I must note that there are plenty of people who love living here, even during the winter, when it is a much more awful place than Scott ever saw.

As for me: Been there, done that, literally got the T-shirt.

- - 30 - -

"Wow, that's tough," Sunny said. "If I were the South Pole, you might hurt my feelings."

"That's why I wanted someone else to read it."

"On second thought, if I were the South Pole, I'd probably call you a wimp and say you're lucky I allowed you to survive."

"All fair. Maybe I should write something different."

"No way. It's raw and honest. We get used to everyone talking about what a wonderful experience this is, and you say it yourself in here, but there's nothing wrong with saying it's difficult and uncomfortable. You say you want my opinion, then my opinion is that you go with it. What's the worst? Someone will say you're a wimp and that he would do better? Fact is he'll never know because he won't ever get to go to Antarctica, much less the South Pole."

"OK, thanks. I value your Gulf Coast opinion and I can put up with any armchair explorer calling me a wimp."

"Hey, it was fun helping."

"Well, actually, there is one other thing I'd like your help with."

DECEMBER 18, 12:10 P.M.

"Thanks for doing this," JP said, sitting next to Sunny in Mac Ops. "Are you sure you're OK with it?"

"There's nothing wrong. Are you like this with all of your secret sources?"

"Maybe my problem is I don't have enough 'secret' sources. Seriously, though, everything is different from the real world down here. At home, if I couldn't get it from someone, I'd file a request under the Freedom of Information Act. We're not in the United States, so I'm a bit insecure."

"Well, I'm secure. You're interested in GASP last season, so I was able to separate all of their communications in chronological order. Let's start at the beginning."

The communications were, by their nature, mundane. JP created his own chart showing how far they traveled each day, their camp locations and various notes.

"You can tell they're in a crevasse zone here because of how they slowed down," Sunny said. "Well, that and the notes that say so. Here, 'advanced only 2 kilometers, slowed by crevasses and weather.'"

What's the problem with the weather? Too cold?"

"Probably blowing snow. Let's see, safe and well with nine souls, wind from 140 degrees at 50 knots. There you go, 50-knot winds. Visibility less than 10 meters, temperature minus 20, so not all that cold."

"Bottom line, you'll move slowly through a crevasse zone when you cannot see 10 meters. How long did that last?"

"To varying degrees, at least three days. It clears here," she said, pointing at the screen. "See, they went only 6 kilometers here but made 89 kilometers the next day with clear skies after clearing the crevasse zone."

"So, where did they lose Shane Peltzer?"

"That was ... well, it was right here, after the 89-kilometer run. An entry was made at 9:58 p.m. of a mayday call, saying a team member was unaccounted for. A SAR team was sounded out at 10:20."

"What was the weather like?"

"Perfect. It's amazing how much it can change in a day. Is any of this helpful?"

"Maybe, but I don't see it. To be fair, I had no idea what might help. At least, I have a better understanding how things flowed. One more thing; how long before they started moving again?"

"They checked back en route after 32 hours, pulling out at 6:07 a.m. with eight souls this time."

DECEMBER 20, 8:30 A.M.

Investigating Peltzer's disappearance was frustrating for JP because it had to take a back seat to everything else. At least, when he was working on a big story back home, he wasn't often handed piddling things to do.

"Not that this work is trivial," he said to himself as he walked toward the helicopter hanger, "and not that I'm actually investigating for a real story. Oh, man, what am I setting myself up for? Am I following Peltzer down that penguin hole?"

He shook his head to remove distracting thoughts and concentrate on his current assignment. Only days since traveling to the South Pole, even before finishing the stories related to that trip, he was taking a helicopter ride to Black Island.

It's only about 25 miles across the sound, but a helicopter was the only practical way to go, particularly with the ice beginning to break up in places as summer closed in. JP was confident Black Island would be an interesting place to visit, but the trip's main attraction was the helicopter ride, something he'd never experienced.

His reason for going was to get photos to go with a story about a new style of satellite dish. The reason for going now was that a spot opened up on a helicopter. The difficult part hadn't been getting a ride to the island as much as it was getting there and back on the same day. So, when the opportunity arose, JP was booked for the trip.

He arrived at the office plenty early, dressed in his ECW and carrying a bag that held extra gear, his hiking boots and camera. Naturally, he had to undergo an orientation.

I wonder if anyone ever flunked orientation, he thought as he failed to maintain focus on the information.

After a little while, his helicopter returned from its first run of the day. JP had long gotten accustomed to the helicopters coming and going. The workhorses of research around the area, they were in constant demand to move cargo and personnel.

He and another rider were told when to approach the craft, wearing the helmets that had been selected to best fit them. The helo tech – helicopter technician – reviewed safety information, saw to it they were correctly buckled in and their helmets connected to the communication system.

The entire process was riveting to JP, but it was obviously old hat for his riding partner. Soon enough, they were taking flight.

Black Island exists as an operations station because of the lack of a crystal ball when the southern tip of Ross Island was selected as the site for McMurdo Station's installation in 1956. Of course, construction actually began there in 1902 with Discovery Hut.

McMurdo's location offered many practical benefits. It's the southernmost point accessible by cargo ships in the late summer, once icebreakers have cleared the path. It's convenient to major penguin and seal colonies, glaciers, sea ice and the one-of-a-kind Dry Valleys. It's also near Mount Erebus, an active volcano that, as volcanoes go, offers amazing possibilities of study.

But Erebus is also the problem. Towering to more than 12,400 feet, it sits north of McMurdo and blocks line of sight with communications satellites in equatorial orbit. Because of the curvature of the planet and the fact McMurdo is so far from the equator, a satellite antenna must be aimed just over the horizon, an angle that found Erebus in the way.

That wasn't an issue in the 1950s, but once satellite communication became a tool around the world, a solution for McMurdo Station was found on Black Island. Satellite antennas there relay signals between McMurdo and the sky.

A Black Island worker – of which there were currently three – signaled in the helicopter and welcomed his two guests, the other of which seemed to be someone of some importance.

Once their bags were dropped inside, another worker guided the reporter to the new satellite dish and answered some questions. With that, JP's primary assignment was knocked out in his first hour on Black Island and he still had six hours to go.

The remainder of the stay was like a weekend back home when he would drive to a small town inland and spend all day visiting shops and the people in them, taking photos and soaking up the town's character.

He had free rein to wander around the island and he used it to give his camera a good workout. He took plenty of photos of the windmills and solar panels that provided most of the electricity for the people and vital equipment. Backup generators made sure things stayed online.

Eventually, he worked his way back inside and spent quite a while visiting with the cook. Like almost everyone on the Ice, she proved a fascinating person with whom to visit. She also served up a great family-style lunch.

After another photography tour of the island, including quite a while sitting on a rock and looking across the ice, the time came to prepare for pickup; one did not want to keep a helicopter waiting.

6 THE PENGUIN HAS LANDED

DECEMBER 22, 10:04 P.M.

"I need my Bubba update," JP said immediately after greetings were exchanged with Jennifer O'Hanlon.

"Your ferret is doing fine, Mr. Weiscarver, and, by the way, so am I. Well, to tell you the truth, he's at Andrea's right now, so I'm assuming he's OK."

"Pardon me, Jennifer. That was rude. I am glad to hear you are well."

"I am great, thank you, but I have been a bit troubled thinking about your puzzle. Should I share? I mean, you called me."

"I just called to chat, so share away."

"Over and over, I've pictured the image of your two guys watching a penguin flop into the water and comparing it to Mr. Peltzer. Then it occurred to me, for him to make that comment and the other guy to shush him, they were both aware of what happened. Unless, again, it was as simple as the first man being habitually rude and the second being sick and tired of him. But, ignoring that possibility, have you considered that maybe the entire team was in on it?"

"No, not really," JP said. "I mean, it's crossed my mind, but I haven't really given it serious consideration. It's possible, of course, but that means seven people would have to keep quiet. You know how difficult that is. Besides, that would also bring the three professors in on it and I just cannot see them risking their careers and their research by killing someone. And why? What's the motive? A thinking person doesn't kill someone just because he's no fun to be with."

"OK, OK, you can just tell me it's a crazy idea."

"I'm sorry ... again. Most likely, I'm mentally exhausted on the topic. Maybe that's why I led off asking about Bubba, an effort to find a simpler, happier topic."

"Oh, JP, I hate that this is eating at you and I hate there is so little you can do about it. Maybe you should try to drop it. Is that possible?"

"I should be able to forget about it. When I pull back and look more objectively, I keep seeing leaps of logic and molehill-sized mountains. I mean, when did I become the Antarctic Police Department? So, let's drop it, at least for now. Tell me what's going on in your world?

"There hasn't been much happening. Everyone seems glad to put more distance between us and the hurricane. Recovery is evident. Christmas is getting even more attention than usual and it's not from marketing. More people seem to be zeroing in on the meaning of Christmas than gifts and decorations."

"There's nothing quite like surviving a horrifying experience to help someone get closer to what's important."

"I read your column on Thanksgiving, which sounded pretty cool. What's Christmas going to be like?"

"The food part, I understand, will be similar to Thanksgiving, but everything else is way different from back home. Quite a few departments have put up fake trees, along with lights and decorations. I'm singing with the Christmas choir. Did I tell you that? We'll perform at the Christmas party, which I believe is more party than Christmas, and at Scott Base; it's been fun."

"That sounds great."

"The biggest difference has been the total absence of commercialization. You know our television here comes through the armed forces. All commercials have been removed, though some have been replaced with information relevant to service members. Also, the only store we have on station isn't pushing Christmas gifts."

"What a relief that would be."

"Thanks, Jennifer, for letting me talk about other stuff."

"I understand. One other thing I wanted to tell you about. I did a little feature story about one of our sheriff's office dispatchers. You mentioned your new friend to me the other day and I thought, for some reason, she might enjoy it."

"Sure. Her name's Sunny and currently she's following in her mother's footsteps as a dispatcher. I'll pass it on to her."

DECEMBER 23, 9:23 A.M.

"Hey, JP, come in," Sunny said with a wave when she spotted him in the doorway. "What brings you into our secret lair?"

"I had to run something by the Chalet, so I took advantage of that to drop this off for you," he said, extending a printout of Jennifer's feature story. Before she could take it, her radio crackled.

"It's your friends from GASP checking in; hold on a second," she said before keying her microphone and turning the sound from her headset to a speaker so JP could hear.

"Foxtrot Sierra Six Three One, this is Mac Ops, over."

"Haven't heard you in a while, Sunny. This is Josh with our daily check-in. We are safe and well with eight souls.

Do your guys need weather info today?"

"They said not, Josh. Guess they're getting a little cocky. You see anything unusual?"

"No, ma'am, just snow everywhere and I guess that should be expected at Christmas."

"Roger that, Josh. Merry Christmas."

She flicked off the speaker and turned toward JP.

"So, there you go."

"Safe and well with eight souls," JP recited.

"Yep, that's what I do, sit here, write down numbers and pass on Christmas greetings."

DECEMBER 23, 12:07 P.M.

JP kept busy at work as lunchtime rolled around and waited for his teammates to leave. He wasn't doing anything wrong, he thought, but he didn't want to face any questions.

He slipped a thumb drive from his pocket, placed it in the computer and copied to it two documents.

"OK, got that for a backup," he whispered. "But let me see if I can find what I want real quick."

First, he opened the current season's Science Planning Summary, or SPS, and searched for GASP. The standardized entry gave a brief synopsis of the program, the principal investigator and her school, and then listed all of the team members deploying to the Ice. He read through the list and recognized all eight names.

"No surprises there. Now to follow my hunch."

He closed that file and opened the previous season's SPS. His gaze went straight to the bottom and the deploying team members: "Principal investigator MaryLu Hatcher, Chris Begin, Marcellus Stapler, Jackson Merkel, Walter Woods, Rick Tomkins, Joshua Smith, Shane Pelzer, and Karen Watkins."

"Nine souls," JP said. "And who are you, Walter Woods?"

DECEMBER 23, 12:27 P.M.

"Jennifer, are you at work yet?"

"No, I was just talking to Bubba. He's fine and appreciates your concern."

"I have a Shane Peltzer assignment for you. Can you write this down?"

"Ready. And, for the record, I never believed you would put this story to rest."

"Neither did I. It occurred to me this morning that when Sunny was reading through last year's log from the GASP traverse the other day that they had nine members in the party and only eight after losing Peltzer. Well, they replaced Peltzer with Terry Masters, but they still have only eight this year."

"Is it unusual for the team's size to change?" she asked.

"Probably not, but I'm not relying on that. I just thought it strange that I've never heard any mention about this ninth person considering how much discussion I've had with numerous people. Anyway, I got his name, Walter Woods, and did an Internet search on him. Come to find out, he's a grad student at the SCAB."

"And you want me to check him out, ask around, is that it?"

"That's not your style, Jen. No, I'd like for you to sit down and have a nice long chat with him."

"I just call him up and tell him I want an interview about his murder of Shane Peltzer?"

"I have you covered there, too. I found online that he's researching erosion patterns on the beach and has been getting into plans to replenish the beaches before next spring. It's just one more post-Clarice story."

"And, should the subject of Mr. Peltzer come up ..."

"He would understand you'll research him and won't be at all surprised that you ask about his time in Antarctica and, should the subject of Mr. Peltzer come up..."

DECEMBER 27, 2:55 P.M.

"I appreciate you coming with me," Jennifer said to Odds and Ends photographer Cole Thompson.

"Hey, it's what I do." They were standing on the beach at the spot designated by Walter Woods. Watching for him was easy since there was hardly anyone else out in the 55-degree weather, rather chilly by local standards.

"I'm not talking about taking the pictures ..."

"Photos."

"I'm not talking about taking the photos," she said, emphasizing the preferred term while punching him in the shoulder, "but hanging around with me."

"And I know you want me to go over my role one more time, either out of fear my brain was recently wiped clean or because you have a strange and overwhelming mommy instinct, so, here goes. I will do my job taking photos and, if he brings someone with him, I'll somehow draw that person away if the conversation gets into Antarctica. However, I will not in any way leave you alone with this Walter Woods. And what will you do?"

"I promise to bring you into the loop as soon as I can."

"Antarctica. Weiscarver's half a world away and he's still messing with me."

"You think that's him?" she asked with a nod toward the parking area.

"My first guess is he's an over-dressed lifeguard who's concerned about our safety." The comment earned him a second punch in the shoulder.

"Mr. Woods," Jennifer said.

"It's Walter, please, and you must be Jennifer. And ..."

"And this is our photographer, Cole Thompson."

"Ah, yes, I've admired your work."

"You're kind," Cole said. "If I understood Jennifer correctly, we're admiring your work on this replenished beach."

She caught his eyes and gave him a smile. He really was

a great partner in an interview.

The questions and answers progressed well. Jennifer was glad she had an interesting story to turn in to Stanley Hopper to cover having two people tied up out here. Oh, well, she thought, it's time to move to phase two.

"Best I could tell, you've just come to State College last summer. What brought you here?"

"I'm working on my doctorate under Dr. Marcellus Stapler. I had started on a different program last fall on the West Coast but changed directions after working with Dr. Stapler last year and decided to move to this coast."

"Yes, I saw you were a member of the GASP team last year. Why aren't you back on the Ice this year?"

Walter looked a little surprised by the question, but then he decided it was not unusual for her to be aware of it due to Stapler's involvement.

"It, uh, it just didn't work out this year," he answered.

Jennifer scribbled in her notebook to stall and it had the desired effect.

"I was studying under Dr. MaryLu Hatcher then and she didn't need me this year."

"What was it like working in Antarctica?" she asked, giving him an opportunity to get comfortable again.

"Amazing, absolutely incredible. I mean, the conditions made it tough, but those same challenges help craft an unbelievable and beautiful environment. It's not unlike the Gulf of Mexico in that it creates things of beauty and yet holds awesome power."

Nice try, Jennifer thought, but I'm not letting you off that easily.

"I understand what you mean. I saw such terrible levels of death and destruction caused by Hurricane Clarice that it's sometimes difficult to even think about it."

Walter nodded in silent agreement, thinking his effort to redirect the conversation had paid off. But the reporter then took up the slack in her line, set the hook and reeled him in.

"But you had already dealt with death, perhaps horrific death, on the Ice, hadn't you?" she said, casually making eye contact with Cole to make sure he was watching.

"I'd rather not talk about that, if you don't mind," Walter finally said.

"Actually, I do mind, Mr. Woods," she said. "You know, I saw victims of the hurricane whose bodies were found half a mile inland, buried under tons of debris, but an untold number of people worked to find every single one of them because each had family who deserved to know what happened and to have the opportunity to bury their loved ones in proper fashion."

"You don't know what you're talking about," Walter said, never looking up.

"Shane Peltzer, as I understand, did not have a lot of buddies on the Ice, but he did indeed have friends who cared for him. More importantly, he had family, people who loved him and who have been trying for a year now to understand why he may have walked away to a cold and miserable death. They deserve to know what happened. They deserve, if at all possible, to have a proper burial."

A great sob rolled out of the young man as he knelt and then sat on the sand.

"I cannot carry this any longer," he finally said.

DECEMBER 27, 5:32 P.M.

JP had been checking his personal e-mail way too often, until 10 minutes ago when he finally received a note from Jennifer: "Success! Call when you can."

Fortunately, Simon and Alexia left for dinner right at quitting time. JP contrived an excuse to hold back. A couple of minutes after they left, he was on the phone, punching in the 36 digits he'd almost memorized.

"I've been on pins and needles all afternoon," he said when Jennifer answered the phone. "Did he do it?"

"Hey, Mr. Hot-Shot Reporter, this is my story to tell

and I'll tell it my way, but I will answer that one question with, 'Yes and no.' Before I tell you more, I want to know something. Do you have a plan for what you're going to do with this information? By that, I mean a plan that doesn't involve you going Wild West on the Antarctic frontier."

"An excellent question, especially since I have a well-prepared answer. I've been doing research. High crimes at U.S. stations in the Antarctic occur in an amazingly small number, but when they do they are under the jurisdiction of the U.S. Attorney in the District of Hawaii, the closest federal court.

"As for law enforcement, there really isn't much. But, when it's needed, the National Science Foundation station manager is a special deputy with the U.S. Marshals Service. I also double-checked and confirmed that our current manager was not on the Ice last summer, so it's unlikely he's complicit in any wrong-doing."

"So you're going to your local marshal with the information and letting him have the shootout at high noon. Right?"

"That's the plan. Now, I'll try to keep quiet and just take notes while you fill me in."

"First of all, the hurricane angle will be pretty good, too. Thanks for that. When I got around to the subject of Shane Peltzer – which I handled quite masterfully, I might say – he eventually welcomed the opportunity to tell the story.

"Walter Woods said he didn't like Peltzer one bit, that nobody on the team did. He confessed to giving him a hard time on occasion but insisted he wasn't the only one to do so."

"Why?"

"They didn't like him; that seemed to be reason enough."

"Sounds like middle school."

"It does. Anyway, they had been especially frustrated

by terrible weather while picking their way through an area with a bunch of holes in the ice and had stopped for the night and he decided to play a joke on Peltzer.

"He said their ice train thingy had a module that most of them slept in, but Peltzer slept alone in the workroom module. Every night after dinner in the living room module ... this all sounds so strange ... Peltzer would leave as soon as he finished eating and go to his room, so to speak. The rest of them usually visited and played cards for a while.

"This is where it gets interesting. Are you still there?"

"Yes ma'am, taking copious notes."

"Good. When they stopped to set up camp, one of the things he said they did was put out flags to help find things in blizzard conditions. He, that is Woods, was the last to enter the living room for dinner and, before he did, he thought it would be funny to move the flags going to the workroom, just to mess with Peltzer. He swears the weather wasn't bad enough to need the flags at that time and he only thought it would make Peltzer mad, which seems to have been his primary objective.

"His story, which he repeated often, is that he forgot about it, that Peltzer did indeed leave an hour or so before the others, and that they retired to the sleeping module without Woods giving it a second thought. He did say conditions had gotten much worse during that time but insisted Peltzer's welfare never crossed his mind. He kept saying they always hassled him and this time was no different.

"The next morning, he said, the weather was perfect and he clearly saw the flags placed in the wrong direction. Before anyone else got outside, he checked on Peltzer without finding him and then quickly pulled the flags before anyone saw where they were."

"Just to clarify, he told you this happened the same day they were in bad weather and around the crevasse zone."

"Yes, without a doubt."

"Sorry to interrupt; please go on."

DECEMBER 28, 8:13 A.M.

JP had insisted on speaking with Patrick Stiles as soon as possible but did not tell him what it was about.

As soon as the name of Shane Peltzer came up, JP felt he had the station manager's attention and the reporter carefully relayed the information on his notepad.

"Where is Walter Woods right now?" Patrick asked and JP handed him a phone number.

"He's supposed to be at home waiting for a phone call. He's agreed to cooperate. I suspect you could call him now; he's probably not sleeping."

"Thank you, JP. I must ask you to keep this under wraps right now. I'd like to make an effort to find the body, which is quite possible with this information, before moving forward."

"Understood," JP said. "I'll share that with my partner stateside and she will keep it mum. I do have one request of my own. May I be there when the arrest is made?"

DECEMBER 30, 10:33 A.M.

"Foxtrot Sierra Six Three One, this is Skier Five Nine making flyby, over."

"Skier Five Nine, this is Foxtrot Sierra Six Three One. We copy you loud and clear and have a landing strip cleared and marked, over."

All eight members of the GASP team watched as the LC-130 aircraft touched down on the ice and turned at the end of the landing strip. By then, four snowmobiles were already carrying the eight campers to the plane.

A member of the flight crew lowered and descended the steps, asking the GASP team to go inside the plane. Marcellus thought the officer carried himself in a more businesslike manner than usual and then noticed what he thought was a sidearm under his coat. One doesn't see guns on the Ice.

Marcellus looked around at his partners and recognized nothing but wonder or confusion among them, except for MaryLu, who was clearly enraged and who followed him up the steps.

When he entered the cargo hold of the plane, he saw just four rows of seats and an otherwise empty belly. Several people were standing at the front watching them enter. The only one he recognized right away was his reporter friend, but the situation did not seem conducive to greetings, so he kept his tongue.

As MaryLu entered the plane, however, her anger exploded.

"I sure hope someone is prepared to lose their job for pulling us off our research in order to play games, or whatever it is you're doing."

"Dr. Hatcher, that would be my job that's on the line," said Patrick Stiles.

"Patrick, you're not one to jeopardize our mission," she said, in a remarkably calmer voice. "Is there something wrong?"

He had them all take a seat on the front row while he flipped through some papers. When he started speaking, he did so slowly while carefully watching the people in front of him.

"Over the last two days, a search-and-rescue team from McMurdo Station located and successfully retrieved the body of Shane Peltzer."

His announcement elicited a slight murmur from some of the team and an audible gasp from Karen, the cook.

After a moment's pause, he held up a color photograph of Peltzer's frozen corpse. That brought stronger reactions. Karen started crying. The men varied with degrees of shock, compassion and curiosity.

MaryLu, again, looked angry.

"What do you want, Patrick?"

The station manager signaled one of the officers to escort Terry Masters, Peltzer's replacement, to the side of the aircraft. His gaze never left the other seven.

"I want to know why members of GASP contributed to the death of Mr. Peltzer. I want to know how you killed him. I would like to know why ... why he's dead and why his family had to wait a year to receive his remains."

Among six of the faces before him he recognized confusion and denial. Only MaryLu displayed any understanding of what was happening. Instead of focusing on her, however, he walked up to Jackson.

"Tell me, Mr. Merkel, who assisted in killing Mr. Peltzer? Everyone? Just you and Dr. Begin?"

"That's not possible," Chris Begin said. "Nobody here had a reason to kill Shane. He was a jerk and no fun to be around, but he did his job without getting in our way. Sure, we'd all have liked to have Terry last year, but nobody killed Shane."

"What about Walter Woods?" asked Rick Tomkins. "Maybe that's the real reason he didn't come back this year. After all, he was always riding Shane more than anyone."

"Do tell, Marcellus," said MaryLu, "is that why Walter left my program and transferred to yours, so he wouldn't have to come back this year?"

"I don't know," Marcellus said. "He told me you drummed him out. No, wait, I do know. You, Dr. Hatcher, you told me you did not want him back on the Ice with us. You questioned his research skills. Or, at least, you said he could not be trusted and maybe I assumed you were speaking of his work."

Patrick had repositioned himself in front of the principal investigator.

"Dr. Hatcher, criminal investigators stateside have talked to Walter Woods. It seems he was dying to unburden his soul about what he knew of Shane Peltzer's death."

"Did he tell you he was the one who killed him? As a joke? Did he tell you he came to me only after Shane was dead?"

"How did you know he was dead?" Patrick asked.

"He had to be. He was gone overnight in blizzard conditions. There's just no way he could have survived."

"Wait," Marcellus cut in. "What do you mean blizzard conditions. The weather was clear and bright."

"Thank you, Dr. Hatcher," Patrick said. "That's what I needed to hear. You've just confirmed that you abandoned a lost man."

Everyone was assembling the pieces at this point.

"Do I understand this correctly?" Chris said. "You knew Shane was missing during that blizzard in the crevasse zone, but you left him there and reported it hours later from a location nowhere near the body. Is that right?"

"Why?" asked Marcellus. "You're a woman of science, of reason. What would justify such an action?"

"Why?" MaryLu finally exploded. "Maybe because I am a woman of science. Maybe for the same reason you cannot get that department head position you want, Marcellus. Maybe for the same reason you cannot win any grants, Chris. Neither of you is willing to put the research first. It's quite possible we would not be here right now, conducting this important research, had I caved in to sentimentality and gone searching for the body of a dead man."

"Did you really know he was dead?" Karen asked. "Maybe we could have found him before he died."

"Logic dictated that he would be dead," MaryLu said. "Did I see the body? No. Was our research more important than him? Most definitely."

Producing a badge, Patrick stated, "Dr. MaryLu Hatcher, you are under arrest on a charge of obstruction of justice and for investigation into the death of Shane Peltzer."

DECEMBER 30, 10:59 A.M.

"I suspect, Mr. Weiscarver, you know more than I about what just happened here," Marcellus said once they were able to speak off to the side.

"I should be free to talk about it now," JP said, aware that he wasn't doing a very good job holding back the satisfaction he felt in seeing the case play out.

"You were asking me questions about Shane all the way back in Oldport. Were you digging into the case even then?"

"Heavens, no. I guess mysteries intrigue me. Actually, my partner at the Odds and Ends pushed me about it early on and then," he said while reaching out to pull Chris Begin and Jackson Merkel into the conversation, "there were these fellows."

"I'm sorry," Chris said, looking back and forth between the others.

"Yes, the two of you provided much of the motivation I needed to continue digging into Peltzer's death."

Chris and Jackson stood waiting while JP milked the anticipation.

"Tell me if this sounds familiar," the reporter finally said. "'Look, he just did a Peltzer.'"

"You jerk," Chris said, slapping Jackson on the back of the head.

"That's exactly what you did when he first said that, when that penguin flopped into the water," JP said when he quit laughing.

"I don't understand how his rude comment led you to connect MaryLu to Shane's disappearance."

"It didn't, really. At first, I was trying to figure out why the two of you would have killed him and I couldn't come up with anything."

"We're really confused here," Marcellus said, "or, at least, I'm confused. Did MaryLu kill Shane? Or did Walter? What happened?"

By this point, all seven remaining GASP members were gathered around.

"Not to be too dramatic," JP said, "but the way I understand it, you all might leave this feeling you played a hand in Peltzer's death. Except Terry, of course. That is, if it's true that you all hazed him to some degree."

He paused only a second while his listeners shifted uncomfortably.

"Walter Woods, it appears, was playing just another practical joke the night Peltzer disappeared, which was the night before you had been led to believe. He moved flags to the workshop module so they led away from the camp instead. He swears conditions were not bad at the time and that he later forgot about it."

"I remember that evening," Karen said. "It did get pretty nasty out."

"The theory is Peltzer followed the flags and got lost. The storm was so bad he made some poor decisions and wandered away from camp. He fell into a small crevasse not far from where you were playing cards. He was wedged in there pretty tightly, from what I heard."

"So, what's Dr. Hatcher's role?"

"Her mistake, it seems, is not reacting appropriately. Woods did not remember his prank until the next morning, he says, and it was then he did not find Peltzer. He confessed to Hatcher and it was her plan to conceal his absence from the rest of you until the end of the day."

"Why would she do that?" Jackson asked.

"To stay on schedule," Marcellus answered. "We were pressing our window last year. Had we lost more than a couple of days, the entire study might have been sacrificed. Implicating a crew member in another's death would likely have brought our trip to a halt."

"What about now?" asked the station manager, who had been quietly monitoring the discussion. "Can the two of you wrap it up without Dr. Hatcher?"

"The seven of us can," answered Chris, looking at

heads nodding around him. "In fact, I'm certain we can do it within our prescribed time frame, barring any prolonged severe weather."

"Then you should get to work," Patrick said. "They're on the way back with Dr. Hatcher and her personal effects and we'll be out of your hair. Let me know if you need anything."

DECEMBER 30, 9:17 P.M.

"It seems strange that we'll be printing a news story here with you supplying much of the information from Antarctica," Jennifer said while petting Bubba.

"There's no reason to play up my role in it," JP said.

"I don't know why not. You solved the case."

"It's more reasonable to say you solved the case, Jen. It was your skillful questioning of Walter Woods that gave us the vital information, particularly that which led to the recovery of Peltzer's body."

"Well, true. Let's just say you and I make one crackerjack team, even separated by half a world."

"I'm sorry, did you just say crackerjack? How old are you? My grandfather is the last person I heard say that."

"Really, Mr. Weiscarver? Then I'd say you need to expand your horizons a bit."

"Said the woman holding a ferret to the man in Antarctica."

"Big deal. Besides, the ferret says it's time for you to come home."

"Six more weeks, Bubba," JP said. "Six more weeks and I'll come rescue you and tell you all about my adventures."

- - 30 - -

ABOUT THE AUTHOR

Steve Martaindale likes to describe his specialization as generalist, saying his interest in many things, even though master of few, proved beneficial as a newspaper reporter and editor. His more than 20 years of working in small daily newspapers has been punctuated with stints as diverse as running a courier service, volunteer firefighter, managing a condominium, delivering flowers, selling souvenirs in a national park and working as a journalist in Antarctica.

That breadth of experience has paid off again as Martaindale transitions from fact to fiction. He draws on associations with a wide range of people to apply reality to his characters and their stories.

He and his wife, Leah, reside wherever they desire and enjoy a daughter, a son-in-law, a grandson and absolutely no more pets.

"The Reporter and the Penguin" is the third of the JP Weiscarver series. The first two – known to Steve simply as "Ferret" and "Hurricane," were published under one cover, "The Reporter, a Ferret and a Hurricane." It is available through Amazon or the author's web site, www.stevemartaindale.com. Keep up with JP Weiscarver and his further adventures by liking his page at facebook.com/JPWeiscarver.

Made in the USA
San Bernardino, CA
22 November 2013